Life is But A Dream

Life is But A Dream

A NOVEL OF SCIENCE FICTION AND FANTASY

SHAND STRINGHAM

LIFE IS BUT A DREAM
A NOVEL OF SCIENCE FICTION AND FANTASY

iUniverse books may be ordered through booksellers or by contacting:

iUniverse
1663 Liberty Drive
Bloomington, IN 47403
www.iuniverse.com
844-349-9409

Because of the dynamic nature of the Internet, any web addresses or links contained in this book may have changed since publication and may no longer be valid. The views expressed in this work are solely those of the author and do not necessarily reflect the views of the publisher, and the publisher hereby disclaims any responsibility for them.

Any people depicted in stock imagery provided by Getty Images are models, and such images are being used for illustrative purposes only. Certain stock imagery © Getty Images.

ISBN: 978-1-6632-6948-5 (sc)
ISBN: 978-1-6632-6949-2 (e)

Library of Congress Control Number: 2024925973

Print information available on the last page.

iUniverse rev. date: 12/27/2024

In Appreciation

I had the assistance and technical support of several talented people in the preparation of this novel whom I want to acknowledge and thank, Karen Westergard Gill, Shellie Stringham Harris, Linda Gareh-Applegate, Isabell and Joseph Stringham, and Robert Smith.

As always, I express my continuing gratitude to my wife, Quin, who spent many hours discussing with me various ideas, concepts, and insights that emerged in the writing of the manuscript. Thank you for your loving support and understanding.

Shand Stringham
Carlisle Pennsylvania
November 2024

Preface

When I was a young man in high school, we read three masterful poems by Edgar Allen Poe, "Annabelle Lee," "The Raven," and "A Dream Within a Dream." Although the first two were perhaps more lyrical, the poem which I appreciated the most was "A Dream Within a Dream." It excited within me a sense of bewonderment about the true nature of dreams and dreaming and the question of whether or not you could actually have a dream within a dream. Now, in my mature years, the poem has inspired me to think back on the question again and write a short novel on the theme. I hope that you enjoy it.

A Dream Within A Dream
by Edgar Allan Poe

Take this kiss upon the brow!
And, in parting from you now,
This much let me avow —
You are not wrong, who deem
That my days have been a dream;
Yet if hope has flown away
In a night, or in a day,
In a vision, or in none,
Is it therefore the less *gone*?
All that we see or seem
Is but a dream within a dream.

I stand amid the roar
Of a surf-tormented shore,
And I hold within my hand
Grains of the golden sand —
How few! yet how they creep
Through my fingers to the deep,
While I weep — while I weep!
O God! Can I not grasp
Them with a tighter clasp?
O God! can I not save
One from the pitiless wave?
Is *all* that we see or seem
But a dream within a dream?

Chapter One

Milton didn't remember much about his younger years. There wasn't really much to remember. He had had a rough time trying to sleep that last night at home. He was wheezing and coughing up mucus and had difficulty catching his breath. He moved into and out of sleep the whole night long. He had a dim recollection that his mother jostled him early the next morning into full wakefulness. He was surprised to hear the rooster in the barnyard crowing to welcome the dawn, and he wondered where the night had gone. His mother hugged him close. Her wet, salty tears rolled down her cheeks and dropped onto his face that he tasted with his tongue.

"Miltie, my love," she sobbed. "I just got a phone call from the hospital clinic. They told me that the tests came back and that you tested positive for the polio virus. They said that it appears to be advanced. They told me to get you into the clinic as fast as I could so they could get you hooked up in a tank respirator… an iron lung… to help you breathe."

Milton's mother was in a state of panic. After listening to Milton cough all through the night trying to breathe, she already realized that what the voice on the other end of the line had said was true. She had read a long article in the weekly newspaper about the rapid spread of the polio virus and she recognized the symptoms. Milton had passed a difficult night breathing as the polio virus gradually paralyzed his chest muscles. If he didn't get treatment soon, there was every possibility that he wouldn't live to see another day.

Milton remembered vaguely his mother bundling him up in a blanket and guiding him out to the family station wagon with her arm wrapped around his shoulders to avoid any possibility of him slipping and falling. She sat him upright in the front seat of the car next to her and anchored him in with a ratchet strap so that she could monitor his breathing as she drove to the hospital.

Two hours later, when they arrived at the entrance to the polio hospital clinic, Milton remembered several orderlies dressed in white lab coats and surgical masks rushing out and laying him out supine on a gurney. They rushed him through the double doors of the clinic down a long corridor into a cavernous bay treatment room where there were long lines of iron-lung canisters set up in rows along each side of the room.

As the orderlies wheeled the gurney to the canister designated for him, it occurred to Milton that it resembled an oversized hot water heater tank like the one in the basement of his home back on the farm, except that the water heater in his basement stood upright on its end. These cylinders in the bay were all arranged in long rows horizontally lying on their side.

He overheard one of the orderlies instruct the other, "Be careful there, Sam. This is your first polio patient. We've got to lay the boy out on the cookie tray and slide it into the cylinder to be calibrated and initiated as fast as we can get it set up and operational."

The orderlies went straight to their work, gently positioning Milton on the padded tray at the end of the iron lung that faced the wall. As soon as they had him laid out flat with his arms at his side and his head resting on a small pillow at the end of the canister, they manually pushed the tray feet first on small rollers into the huge canister. They quickly closed the hinged, double doors leaving Milton's head protruding out of the canister resting on the outside pillow tray. They next ran some tests to make sure that there was a good seal around Milton's neck without obstructing his airways. Then they turned on the machine's air compressor system, and the iron lung started to expand and compress the air inside the cylinder, forcing air in and out of Milton's weakened lungs.

Once the orderlies had completed their work, the two young men walked around to the end of the canister where Milton's head rested on the pillow. "How are you doing now, Miltie? Is that easier for you to breathe?"

The two orderlies were upbeat, obviously trying to make Milton more comfortable with his plight. They stood in his limited field of vision so that he could focus and see them. They were both wearing surgical masks which disguised their faces. One was tall and slender and the other was shorter and stocky.

Milton coughed and wheezed for a few moments clearing phlegm from his lungs, and then he slowly formed a question: "Do I know you guys? How do you know my name?"

The tall orderly laughed and responded, "No, my friend. We just met as we carried you in from your mother's car at the clinic entrance. Your name is printed on a cardboard plaque above your head at the top of your iron lung. It reads 'Milton Jeffries... but please call me Miltie.' Is that right, you want us to call you Miltie?"

"Yes"... cough... cough, "that's what everyone calls me. What're your names"

"The tall orderly responded, "My name is Jack." The shorter orderly chimed in, "and my name is Sam. Good to meet you, Miltie. Glad to see that you can talk okay. Remember to talk when you expel air with the help of the machine. Don't try to talk when it is expanding your chest cavity and filling your lungs with air. That doesn't work very well...It could even hurt a little. We hope that this contraption makes it easier for you to breathe as you heal from the virus."

"It seems to help some... What is it anyway?... How does it work?"

Sam, the shorter orderly, spoke right up, "It's called an iron lung. Some folks who have been here for quite some time refer to it as an 'iron maiden,' but the correct name is simply an 'iron lung.' It uses a principal of negative pressure to assist your lungs with breathing. The polio virus has destroyed the muscles that cause your lungs to work properly. Since they have been seriously compromised, this iron lung creates a partial vacuum around your body using negative pressure that causes your chest to expand

and inflate your lungs. Then the negative pressure is released allowing your lungs to exhale. And then the process keeps on repeating itself. Just relax and let the iron lung do your breathing for you. Don't fight the rhythm of the pump... just relax and breathe with the rhythm of the machine... air in... air out... air in... air out."

"Even with my lungs clearer, it's still difficult to talk."

"I can imagine so." Sam acknowledged. "Remember not to struggle against the rhythm of the machine... air in... air out. You'll only be able to speak without difficulty when you exhale, pretty much the way all of us normally talk, forcing the passage of air past your vocal cords. When the pump pulls the air from the inside of the tank, it causes your lungs to expand, but as your lungs expand, it makes it pretty difficult to talk.

Milton attempted to process all of this technical information he was learning about his new mechanical domain. He was familiar with the use of pumps from his work on the farm. "How does this pump operate? Where does it get its power?"

This time Jack, the tall orderly, chimed in with a response. "The pump runs on electricity. It's pretty reliable and shouldn't cause you any grief."

"What happens if the power goes off like it does back on the farm? Does that mean that the pump will stop working and I'll die?"

"Oh no, not at all. Should we lose power, we'll be alerted by an alarm bell and we'll come and keep the pump doing its job using a small hand crank at the other end of the tank. We've never had to use it yet, but we're trained and prepared should the need present itself."

Milton considered what he had just learned, and realized that he had no control over his breathing. The iron lung had begun expanding and contracting the air flow on the inside of the canister when it was activated, and began the mechanical task of doing the majority of his breathing for him.

Jack, the tall orderly, was apparently in charge. "Not very comfortable, Miltie?" he asked with genuine concern in his voice. He tried to assist Milton in getting comfortable. There were hinged portal doors and windows running down each side of the canister tank. The two orderlies opened the hatch doors to access Milton's frail body and adjust his limbs and applied hot packs to treat his pain.

With the doors open, it broke the seal into the tank and the breathing apparatus didn't function as well. Milton had a much harder time trying to breathe. While the doors were open, Jack helped Milton locate a call button hanging from the top of the interior canister wall that he could use to call for help when he needed it. They worked fast and then closed the access doors again as quickly as possible. They were intent on making him comfortable while allowing the iron lung to do its job.

"Does the pump always stop functioning when you open the hatch on the side of the canister like you just did?" Milton asked.

Jack continued his spiel on the workings of the machine. "No, Miltie, not entirely. The pump continues to function, although not as effectively as when there is a complete vacuum inside the tank. You don't suffer any undue risks when we open the side hatch to help adjust your body and apply hot packs to ease the pain. When we close the hatch, the machine goes back to full functionality."

When they finished shutting and sealing the side access doors, the iron lung continued pumping as before, and Milton could tell the difference when there was a full vacuum in the tank. As he shifted around in the tank trying to find a more comfortable position, Milton suffered a minor claustrophobic attack. His body lay on the bed tray entirely enclosed inside the oversized metal canister and it greatly restricted his movement. He felt like the huge machine was smothering him. He twisted and turned, still trying to find a comfortable position, but after several frustrating efforts, he finally gave up and just lay there, tensed up and immobile. As the orderlies turned to leave, Jack turned back to the side of the iron lung and spoke reassuringly to Milton, "If you need anything, Miltie, just press on the red button hanging down on the wire near your head. One of us will be back in a heartbeat to help you."

As the orderlies left, Milton started to panic and he shouted out, "My mom… where's my mom?"

"Don't you worry, Miltie," Jack responded. "She's out in the waiting room. I'll go get her and escort her back here to see you."

The orderly disappeared momentarily and reappeared with Milton's mother in tow. The orderly led her around to the head of the canister so that Milton could see her. She immediately began to tear up when she saw Milton encased in the iron canister. She was distraught that Milton looked so miserable and vulnerable with just his head exposed.

"Are you alright, Miltie?" she managed to eke out. "Can you breathe okay in there?"

Milton felt comfortable enough lying on the thin mattress on the cookie tray. Psychologically, he was actually quite miserable, but he managed to put on a brave face when he saw how overwrought his mother was. She remained by the side of Milton's iron lung for almost an hour, rumpling his hair, caressing his face, and conversing quietly. Finally, looking down at her wristwatch, she looked over at Milton and said her tearful goodbyes. She had a long two-hour drive back to the farm, and she faced a myriad of chores that she needed to accomplish before she and Milton's father could lie down and rest for the night.

After his mother departed, Milton realized that he had to go to the bathroom and that he had been holding it in far too long. But he didn't have a clue about how to go about it. Then he remembered Jack's instructions and pushed the red button dangling on the wire beside him. Jack and Sam were there at his side in a flash.

"What's happening, Pardner?" Sam quipped with a big grin on his face.

Milton squirmed and responded, "I've got to take a leak."

"Not a problem, Ol' Buddy," Jack chimed in. "We've got just the ticket for that."

He reached over to the tray suspended on the side of Milton's iron lung and retrieved a metallic gray urinal. He undid the side window latch on Milton's iron lung and opened the hatch, pushing the urinal through and up to Milton's side. "All you have to do, Miltie, is turn to your side a bit and pee into this bottle. I'll steady it while you use it so you don't get pee all over. Tell me when you're done and I'll take it out and empty it in the latrine."

Milton did his business and then asked, "What do I do if I want to go number two?"

Jack laughed. "Logical question. Same answer… almost. Just press the red button and when Sam and I come, just tell us you have to defecate and we'll fetch you the bedpan."

"Defecate? What does that mean?"

"Pardon me, Miltie. It means "take a dump,"… you know… 'number 2.' When you tell us that, Sam will assist me as we open the hatch door and, while Sam helps you elevate your midsection in the air, I'll slide the bedpan in under you. Then, just take care of business. When you're done, we'll remove the bedpan to empty it, and Sam or I will help clean you up."

"Clean me up? You mean wipe my butt?"

"That's about it my friend. After a while, you'll get expert at all this and you'll be able to do most of it yourself without much help from Sam and me."

After the two orderlies left, Milton just lay there on the cookie tray in his iron lung breathing slowly with the rhythm of the bellows moving the air into and out of his lungs. He was frightened that he might have to spend a long time in his iron prison. That realization was terrifying for him and he tried to put the thought out of his mind. He tossed and turned in a limited, constricted way, dreaming short bursts of frightful dreams and nightmares that robbed him of restful sleep. Finally, after several hours of fitful visions, he finally drifted off to a deep, but unrestful sleep.

During the next few weeks, Milton gradually fell into a routine with his orderly attendants coming by every morning precisely at 8:00 a.m. to reach through the glass access panel doors to give him a massage and adjust his body position so he didn't get bed sores. It took a lot of getting used to for Milton to tolerate that much attention. Initially, he hated every minute of it, but as time went by, Milton grew to appreciate their ministrations.

Milton had been coughing and wheezing hard, trying to clear the phlegm from his lungs when his mother delivered him to the clinic. But the iron lung performed its mechanical task well, and Milton was soon able to breathe without coughing and hurting. Much as he hated being cooped up in his cylindrical prison, he realized that it was probably what was keeping him alive.

Time passed. He lay there immobilized in the iron lung for what seemed like weeks. Milton eventually lost track of exactly how many. It all dissolved into a hazy blur over time.

There weren't any windows in the long bay wall nor any wall clocks that he could see from where his iron lung was positioned, and he couldn't monitor the passage of time. He didn't have much to keep him entertained. He couldn't hold a book or turn pages, and there wasn't a television in the bay. Back home on the farm, Milton's family had just purchased a black and white console TV, and Milton already had a list of favorite programs that he liked to watch in the evening and on weekends when he finished his farm chores. He missed that! There was a network radio playing popular tunes softly in the background, but it quickly became repetitive and boring for him, and there were days when he wished that he could just block it out.

His dreams never did settle down to restful sleep. They were frightful nightmares that recalled some of the worst experiences of his life… getting trampled by a big cow he was trying to milk in the barn, and running away from a charging bull across the south pasture that was intent on his demise. His worst nightmare occurred shortly after he arrived at the polio clinic. He awoke in the night, half asleep, with the sensation of a giant cockroach crawling across his face, and he couldn't use his hands or arms inside the iron lung to brush it away. His fear got the better of him, and he let out a loud scream that echoed off the walls of the cavernous bay.

Both Jack and Sam came running, fearing the worst for Milton. They found him shivering and shaking, still caught up in a half-sleep, bad dream. Jack opened the side hatch and shook Milton gently.

"What's wrong buddy? You're all in a cold sweat."

Milton had a hard time catching his breath… trying to breathe with the beat of the iron lung pump, but he failed miserably and was breathing with little regard for the rhythm of the big machine. Gasping for breath, he blurted out, "It was a giant cockroach crawling across my face. It was horrible."

Both Jack and Sam quickly looked around to see if there was indeed a giant insect, but they didn't find anything.

"It looks like you were having a bad dream… a very bad dream, Miltie. Are you okay now? Are you going to be able to go back to sleep? Would you like one of us to stay here with you until you drift off?"

Milton realized that the orderlies were trying to be helpful, but he didn't want them to think that he needed to be watched like a baby.

"No… no thanks guys. I think that I'll be okay now. Thanks for coming so fast. I'm sorry if I woke up everyone else in the bay."

"Think nothing of it, Miltie. Practically everyone who comes here has an episode with an ultra-realistic nightmare. It just goes with the territory."

Jack went and fetched a wet washcloth and wiped the sweat off Milton's forehead. "Does that help, Miltie?"

"Yes, a little. Thanks."

Jack and Sam stood there in silence for a few minutes more making sure that Milton was okay, and then they turned in unison and walked back toward their lab station where they could monitor and respond to the entire wing of the building.

As they exited the bay, Jack turned to Sam and asked quietly, "What was that all about? Our patients rarely have nightmares. Why did you tell Miltie that they do?"

Sam smiled a grim smile and opened a towelette he had scrunch up in his hand. "Because of this, ol' buddy."

In the middle of the scrunched up towelette, Jack could see an indeterminate black mass. "What's that? I can't tell."

"It's the carapace of a very large cockroach. I found it on the floor over in the corner next to the baseboard when we were looking around."

"Okay, biology wasn't my strong suit in my undergraduate studies. What is a carapace?"

"A carapace is essentially the body armor plate for a cockroach, a critter that has been around for millions of years. We've got a problem... a serious problem. Miltie wasn't dreaming. He probably woke up with a giant cockroach crawling across his face."

"Well, I've got something to confess... When we came rushing into the bay, I thought I saw a large black insect crawling on the wall beside Miltie's iron lung, but as I looked at it, trying to focus, to see it more clearly, it simply disappeared into thin air. One second it was there... the next moment it was gone."

"You think that Miltie had it right? There was a giant cockroach there and it probably scampered across his face. Miltie's scream sent it running up the wall."

"Yes. All right. Except that it didn't get away in the normal sense. It simply disappeared as it ran up the wall. I checked out the wall while we were there, and it's completely smooth... no cracks or holes where the critter could have escaped."

"Whew! I couldn't deal with a big bug crawling on my face while I was asleep, especially with my hands and arms immobilized inside an iron lung. What are we going to do?"

"Only one thing we can do. We need to notify the head resident here in the facility that we may have an infestation of cockroaches... They could be hiding in the wall or congregating in the basement. They're going to need to bring a fumigator here in the facility muy rápido, amigo, to chase them down and eliminate them. And the fumigator has to do it unobtrusively so that our patients don't catch on. Tall order!"

"I'll say! Let's get on it now. I think that Dr. Frederick, the head resident, may be working on paperwork in his office. Let's go deliver the bad news."

⁓

Nick, the fumigator, showed up later that morning. He had been carefully briefed about not being too demonstrative with his work. The goal was to not excite the polio patients about cockroaches.

The fumigator worked for several hours pulling the baseboard back away from the wall and using a small mirror system to look in all directions inside the wall. He didn't find anything. He shrugged and asked the orderlies to show him the access stairs to the basement and the attic. He worked for several more hours inspecting the usual places that cockroaches hide out. Nothing. He didn't see any roaches nor find any signs that there ever had been roaches there.

After almost a full day's investigative work, he reported to Dr. Frederick's office to convey his findings.

"Couldn't find a thing, sir. This building appears to be clean as a whistle. You're doing a great job on cleanliness and maintenance. I wish that all of the buildings they call me to work on were as clean and devoid of roaches as this one."

Dr. Frederick smiled, more than a little perplexed. He held out a corked lab beaker with the cockroach carapace inside. "Then how do I explain this?"

The fumigator took the beaker and held it up to the light. "Well, sir, it's definitely a cockroach carapace, but one like I've never seen before."

"What do you mean?"

"Well, Doc, it looks like it might be a regular cockroach carapace, but there are several parts of it that don't look quite right. Would you mind if I borrowed this and ran it by a biology professor friend over at the university to have him take a gander at it?"

"Not at all. I'd really like to get to the bottom of this. We can't afford having cockroaches running around a polio clinic. They could cause major problems... Aside from creating great unrest among our patients, they could turn out to be Polio's Typhoid Mary that spreads the virus even farther than it's already reached."

The phone on the chief resident's desk rang a few hours later. "Hello, Dr. Frederick. This is Nick... the exterminator. I'm over at the university in Dr. Kim's office. He examined the carapace in the beaker and wants to take it out and put it under a microscope. He says that a cursory examination suggests something odd."

"Odd... like what?"

"Here, Doc, let me put Dr. Kim on the phone."

"Hello, Dr. Frederick. I really appreciate Nick bringing over your cockroach carapace specimen. It is most unusual. It may be one of a kind."

"What do you mean, Dr. Kim?... 'one of a kind?' Cockroaches have been around for millions of years."

"Not the one that sported this carapace. I did some specialty research awhile back, and I'm pretty familiar with what constitutes a normal cockroach in all its myriad versions. This one is different."

"Different? How?"

"On about 14 different points of divergence of normal cockroach exoskeleton structure. If I had to classify it, I would adjudge that it's not really a cockroach... at least not like the ones that have populated the Earth for several million years. It's that different. Would you mind if I held on to it for a while and had several colleagues, specialists in the field, examine it and see what conclusions they draw?"

"Be my guest, but be advised, it may have been exposed to the polio virus. You'll need to treat your specimen with some kind of disinfectant or antiseptic to ensure that we don't run the risk of spreading the polio virus around."

Chapter Two

And so, Milton's 14-year-old life… that had promised so much just a few weeks ago… became an unpleasant exercise in doing nothing but labored breathing and just trying to stay alive. It was so boring for him that he subconsciously began counting the rhythmic beats of the pump as it moved air back and forth in the chamber, keeping his chest muscles active and moving. "Like watching paint dry," Milton said out loud to no one in particular. "Just like watching paint dry. I'd rather be shoveling manure out in the cow stalls back on the farm."

Then one day, two female orderlies wheeled in another gurney with a patient stretched out under a white blanket. They backed it into the space next to Milton's canister and carefully lifted their patient onto the cookie tray and slid her efficiently into the bowels of the adjoining iron lung. Closing the double hinged doors, leaving their patient's head protruding from the canister next to Milton's, they hooked up all the wires and tubes, and quickly went down a checklist on their clipboard ensuring that the system was set up correctly. Satisfied that all was in place, they hit the switch to activate the internal bellows that did the breathing for the patient.

Milton didn't have a lot of strength in his neck muscles at this point, but he was able to turn his head just enough to eyeball his new 'roommate' from afar. He was awestruck! She was a beautiful goddess! Although Milton was barely fourteen years old at the time, he felt an immediate attraction for the newcomer. Her freckles and honey blonde hair took his breath away. He instantly fell in love in a juvenile sort of way.

When the orderlies finished their work and went on to their other clinical duties, Milton lay there on his back trying to work up the courage to initiate a conversation with the beautiful newcomer. Finally, when he could hear that her coughing was letting up some and her breathing had settled down into a healthier rhythm than when they first wheeled her in, Milton attempted a friendly greeting, "Hello there, my name is Milton, but everyone just calls me Miltie."

Milton could hear the girl struggling to get her air passages clear so that she could respond. She coughed and wheezed for several minutes more before she was finally able to talk. Her words came out sporadically, "Oh, that hurts so much... Hello... My name... is... Abigail." There was a long pause. "I was just diagnosed with the... polio virus... and Father rushed me here to the clinic."

"Same for me Abigail. It all happened so fast!"

"How long have you been here?"

"I'm not really too sure. I lost track of time a while back. I think I've been here at least a month or so."

"Oh, that's not good. I'm so sorry for you. I hope that I don't have to stay here that long. My father told me that some people are in and out of here in a couple of weeks." Abigail struggled to say more, but her throat gurgled up with phlegm, and she couldn't get it clear.

Milton was having a difficult time himself carrying on the conversation. His chest hurt with trying to keep the air flowing through his lungs as the bellows moved the air in and out. "I have an idea, Abigail. I'm kind of hurting and it sounds like you are hurting too. Let's give it a rest for now."

Abigail replied, "Thanks... Miltie, I appreciate... your... concern. I could use a nap... right now... myself."

Both of them subsided into a quiet contemplation of the extraordinary turn of events in their lives. Milton was most definitely smitten with Abigail. And it appeared that she was glad to have Milton's company as well. They lay there on the cookie trays in their iron canisters, silently considering their plight, until they both drifted off to sleep.

Chapter Three

Milton didn't have sufficient head and neck mobility to turn his head and view all of the denizens of his iron lung ghetto. But Abigail's canister was positioned immediately to his right, and he could turn his head just enough while lying within the confines of his metal prison to sometimes look at her as they conversed. Milton soon discovered that Abigail was fifteen, just a couple of months older than him. It helped Milton immeasurably to have a fellow inmate nearby as attractive as Abigail and nearly the same age.

To avoid the pain of craning their heads to the side for long stretches of time while they talked, they frequently just lay there in their iron cages staring up at the ceiling and chatting about things that had captured their interest in their young lives.

Granted, they didn't really have much life experience and they didn't have a broad understanding of the world they had left behind when they were brought to the polio treatment and recovery facility. But each of them brought with them a remarkably different menu of childhood memories and perspectives on life. Milton would lie there enthralled as Abigail would describe her previous life so different from his own.

Milton's family were dairy farmers in a rural area upstate where they lived, and most of his early childhood experiences were wrapped up in animal husbandry-related activities... helping his father with milking cows and feeding chickens and other farm livestock. He enjoyed his 4H project raising a pet bull and showing him at the state fair last summer, but Milton's assessment was that his life was pretty dull stuff... nothing much to get excited about remembering as he lay there on the cookie tray in his iron prison.

In contrast, Abigail's family lived and worked in a big metropolitan city. Abigail's father, Herbert Drexel, was a wealthy industrialist. Abigail's mother had died of cancer during the past year and her father now doted on her. He was quite wealthy and ran a big corporation, so it was hard for him to carve out the time to come and visit her. But he dutifully came and visited her every weekend without fail.

Abigail's tales of her family taking long walks through majestic canyons of tall skyscrapers that stretched upwards into the sky and playing in the lush green park in the center of the city excited Miltie's imagination. He was especially fascinated by Abigail's stories about her canoeing adventures on the lake that spread out over a corner of the park.

Occasionally, the technicians at the facility had to work through the side access panels to perform basic maintenance tasks on the iron lungs such as changing the bed linens and switching out the thin mattress for the cookie tray. They set up portable screens on rollers so that their patients had a modicum of privacy. They had to work fast so that Milton and Abigail weren't without the machine's full mechanical breathing effectiveness for any extended length of time. The attendants were mostly friendly young men and women who Milton found out were working their way through medical school.

One day, the doctors who came by from time to time to check up on Milton's progress, informed him that he had been selected for a special program in which they were testing new equipment, medicines, and procedures for minimizing the lingering effects of the polio virus after it had been eliminated from his body.

One of the first changes they introduced into Milton's recovery program was a newly-designed, iron lung canister. It was a much bigger chamber. It had more access panels, wires, buttons and blinking lights, than the previous model that Milton had occupied. The new iron lung wasn't entirely round like he remembered the water heater in his basement back home. Milton assessed that it was slightly elongated and smashed flat on the top and the bottom and looked like the tanker trucks that traveled up and down the highway near his home hauling fuel oil to the outlying farms. His doctor told him that the new tank's shape was called an ovoid... slightly oval in its cross section from one end to the other, and was designed to give him more room to move about to get more comfortable and to do strengthening exercises within the confines of the canister.

What Milton liked most about the new iron lung was that it made his breathing much easier. He wasn't precisely sure why that was so, but it was definitely easier to breath.

One other thing that changed with the new regimen was that a charge nurse came by his canister every day to give him an injection of a new experimental drug. After she had finished with Milton, she moved next door and administered an injection to Abigail as well. They both learned to hate the needle, and although the experimental drug seemed to help their condition to improve, they always dreaded hearing the rolling cart of the charge nurse coming through the bay doors and wheeling it down to where they lay.

Milton's mother came to visit him with great regularity... at least once a week on Sunday mornings. His father only came occasionally. His responsibilities on the farm kept him far too occupied to make the two-hour one-way trip from the farm to the polio treatment and recovery facility in the city.

One day, his mother broke the Sunday morning routine and came to visit Milton three days early on Thursday afternoon. She edged into the lab and slowly approached Milton's new iron lung. When she came into his field of view at the head of his canister, he could see that she had been crying. Her eyes were all red and puffy, and she spoke haltingly through clenched teeth, ostensibly trying to keep her emotions in check and not crying in front of her son. But after a few tense minutes, she finally broke down sobbing uncontrolledly. It took her several more minutes for her to regain her composure.

When she could finally speak, she confided, "Miltie, you are probably wondering why your father hasn't come to visit you in quite a while. Initially, it was because of the long hours he spent bringing in the fall harvest. But, as he was finishing up the last hay baling and stacking the bales in the barn, a tall stack got away from him and tumbled over, crushing him underneath. When I heard the ruckus in the barn, I ran from the house to see what was the matter. When I got to the barn, I saw bales were scattered everywhere in disarray, and I could see your father's legs sticking out from under a jumbled stack. I worked as fast as I could to pull the heavy bales off him, but by the time I had them cleared away, he was already gone. One of the bales had broken several ribs which apparently impaled his lungs, and he couldn't breathe. He simply ran out of breath, and he passed away right there on the floor of the barn."

"Dad is dead?" Milton whispered. The news hit him hard and he started gasping for breath.

"Yes, Miltie. I'm sorry to have to tell you. We held a graveside service at the church cemetery earlier this week. All of our friends from church gathered to pay their respects, and then the menfolk came to our farm with their harvesting equipment to work together to bring in the crops that were still in the field. I couldn't have done it all without them. They're good people, Miltie… mighty good folks."

Milton was still very young to understand all of the nuances of his family losing its primary breadwinner, but he knew intuitively that the future wouldn't look promising for his family down the road.

"With your father gone, Miltie, I'm going to have to pick up the responsibility for the entire farm operation, milking the cows and all. That means that I won't be able to break away quite so often to come here to see you. I hope you understand. I'm going to miss our frequent Sunday visits."

Milton was numb by this point. He knew that he should be comforting his mother with reassuring hugs and kisses, but he was entirely incapable of doing that ensconced as he was in his iron prison.

His two assigned orderlies, Jack and Sam, had been standing to the side witnessing the touching scene. The hospital administrator had already made them aware of Milton's father's passing. When they saw how Milton and his mother were struggling, Sam had an idea. He disappeared for a few minutes and then returned carrying an enamel basin of hot soapy water and set it down on the lip of the external tray that they used when they were attending to Milton.

Jack approached Milton's mother and motioned to her to follow him to the side of the canister. He handed her the soapy washcloth and asked her to wash and sterilize her hands. Meanwhile, as Milton's mother was drying her hands on a towel, Sam opened one of the side glass hatch doors near the top of the canister and invited her to reach in and squeeze Milton's hands. When Milton realized what was happening, he too finally allowed the dam to burst and he broke down sobbing as well. Milton and his mother clasped hands for several minutes, squeezing out messages of love.

And then, his mother abruptly withdrew her hands and washed them again in the basin in the soapy water and walked around to the head of the canister as she dried them. "I'm sorry, Miltie, but I need to be going to get back to the farm to milk the cows on schedule before it gets too dark this evening. It's a long drive and I've got to leave now to beat sundown and the evening traffic."

"I understand, Mom," Milton whispered. "You better hurry. Drive carefully on the long trip home." Milton paused for a moment to catch his breath and then continued, "I can't wait until I can leave all of this behind, and get back to help you out on the farm. I need to be there to carry on with Dad gone now."

Milton's mom nodded but couldn't speak. She simply turned and walked toward the door at the far end of the bay with Jack and Sam holding onto her arms keeping her steady. As they passed through the bay door, she paused and looked up at her two benefactors. "That's right... isn't it? Miltie is getting better and will be able to come home again soon? That's right, isn't it?"

Just then Dr. Frederick came hurrying down the hall in time to hear Milton's mom's plaintive question. Before either of the two orderlies could respond, the doctor spoke softly to Milton's mother, "I'm sorry to have to tell you this, Mrs. Jeffries. Although Milton's condition has stabilized, the tests show that he doesn't appear to be improving. He may need to take up permanent residency here in our clinic for now until he licks the virus and regains strength in his chest muscles."

Milton's mother turned pale with that news. "You mean that he won't be able to come home again for a very long time?"

"That unfortunately may be about right. We don't really know how long his healing process is going to take. It's different for everyone who contracts the polio virus. In point of fact, he may not heal at all and remain crippled or confined to an iron lung for the rest of his life. For all we know at this time, he may still be contagious with the polio virus. We do know that, for now, he's not going anywhere anytime soon."

Taken aback by the new information, Milton's mother broke down again in a flood of tears as the two orderlies stayed by her side escorting her to the outside double doors of the clinic to her car.

Back in the iron-lung bay, Abigail spoke up trying to console Milton. "I heard it all, Miltie. I'm so sorry about your father dying. That's got to be hard for you and your mother. Is there anything I can do or say to help?"

Milton turned his head and looked over at Abigail. She looked to him like an angel stretched out there in her iron lung. "Thanks, Abigail. Just talk to me for a while. It's nice to have you here close by."

Chapter Four

Life went on for Milton… lying there on the cookie tray inside his iron prison. Abigail was a Godsend for him… lifting his spirits with her laughter and pleasant conversation. Milton's mother was true to her word and came to visit him as often as her work on the farm would allow. Her visits were always a special joy for Milton because she reminded him of his old life on the farm and togetherness with his family.

Milton and Abigail were conversing in their canisters on their backs one afternoon when Dr. Frederick entered the bay and walked slowly down the row of canisters to Milton's iron lung. He had a dour look on his face. He paused at the head of Milton's iron lung and looked down on him without speaking, as if he were searching for something to say. Finally, he broke the silence with words that froze Milton's heart. "Miltie, I'm sorry to be the bearer of more bad news, but we just received word that your mother was in a terrible car pileup accident on the north loop highway while driving down from the farm to visit you today."

Milton interrupted in shock, "How is she, Dr. Frederick? How's my mom? Is she okay?"

Dr. Frederick shook his head. "No, Miltie, I'm afraid not. She didn't survive the crash. She died a few hours later in the hospital ER where they took her when they were finally able to extricate her body from the wreckage of the cars."

When Milton realized that his mother had also died, he wanted to scream, but the air just wouldn't come. And so, he just lay there, helpless to do or say anything. With his mother gone, he was now orphaned… abandoned… without parents or other relatives to look out for him and care about him It was just more than he could bear. Milton swiveled his head around and looked over at Abigail. She was crying… her eyes were wet with tears. She mouthed the words, "I'm so sorry, Miltie. I'm so sorry."

Milton appreciated her consoling words. Other than his orderly team, Jack and Sam, Abigail was the only friend he had left in the world now.

Dr. Frederick was sitting in his office hunched over his desk reviewing budgetary figures for the next quarter when the telephone rang. "Hello, this is Dr. Frederick."

"Hello, sir. This is Dr. Kim. We spoke several weeks ago about a peculiar cockroach carapace that my friend Nick, the exterminator, brought in for me to examine.

"Yes, Dr. Kim. I remember you well. Have you found out any additional information about the carapace?"

"Yes, I have, Dr. Frederick. But it is still most puzzling. I took the carapace with me to a professional conference where a group of fellow biologists who specialize in entomology, and more specifically in the study of cockroaches and scarab beetles, were gathered together to listen to several papers."

"Did they get an opportunity to study the carapace I gave you?"

"Yes, sir, they did. In fact, we spent several hours examining every aspect we could think of to classify the cockroach that the carapace came from. But we failed. We simply couldn't agree on its provenance. It is unlike any variety of cockroach any of us had ever seen. Several of my venerable colleagues were uncertain that it was even a cockroach. After all, there are approximately 4,600 species of cockroaches in the world today, and the scientists in that select group at the conference were familiar with most of them to one extent or another. Many of them proposed that it was probably a new species of cockroach, and several suggested that it might even be a new genus."

"I had no idea that cockroaches were that diverse in the world."

"Oh, but they are, Dr. Frederick. My colleagues were most interested in knowing how you came into possession of such an interesting variant."

"Yes, of course. One of our patients in an iron lung woke up screaming that there was a giant cockroach crawling on his face. My interns did an immediate search of the area and found the carapace on the floor underneath his iron lung, but they never did see the cockroach that shed it. The exterminator worked all the next day, but didn't turn up evidence of any cockroaches at all." "When doing my rounds not long after the incident, I took it upon myself to interview the patient to see if he could throw some light on the matter. He told me that that night, he was having a bad dream, a real nightmare, that included being overrun by a bunch of cockroaches on his farm."

"Intrusion of cockroaches... that's what you call a bunch of cockroaches," Dr. Kim advised.

Dr. Frederick nodded and continued, "Our patient said that the nightmare was so frightening and real that it woke him up to find a cockroach crawling across his face. The cockroach apparently scampered away when he screamed, and we never did see it again."

"Hmmn, that's most interesting. Please call me if you ever have another cockroach sighting there at the clinic."

"That I can do, Dr. Kim. I hope that I never have to call you about... an intrusion... of roaches again."

A few weeks later, Jack and Sam came by one morning to inform Milton that they had completed their clinicals for med school and would be moving on to their next professional assignment. They brought by the two new orderlies who would replace them in the polio bay, Frank and Ernie. They seemed nice enough, but Milton reasoned it would take some time to get used to them and establish a working bond to take over all the intimate chores that Jack and Sam had performed… chores like sponge baths, bed linen changes, and assistance with urinals and bedpans.

And then, when it seemed like his life couldn't be any deeper and darker in upheaval, Milton woke up early one morning to find that the iron lung next to his was now vacant, and Abigail was gone… she was no longer there. Milton pressed the red button to summon the orderlies. It took them a little longer than usual to get to his tank.

"Morning, Miltie. How's it going?" Frank asked. "Did you get a good rest last night?"

"Yeah, pretty much… but that's not why I called you. What happened to Abigail, the girl in the next iron lung over? She's not there now" And then he continued cautiously, expecting the worst… "Did she die during the night?"

"Oh no," Ernie responded with a laugh. "Nothing quite so awful or dramatic as that. The polio committee here at the center met last evening and decided that her condition had improved greatly. Tests showed it appeared that her polio was in remission and they decided to transfer her to the transition wing of the clinic to help her prepare to return home to normal life and be with her father full time."

"You mean…" Milton sputtered… "She's all well now?"

"Well, not quite, Miltie," Ernie broke in. "Her polio infection has left her breathing slightly impaired, and her leg muscles are atrophied. But her body no longer shows any sign of the virus. She's going to have to do a lot of physical therapy and muscle exercises to get back on her feet. That may take a while, but she should pull through it just fine."

Milton was totally depressed and asked expectantly, "Do the tests show that I'm improving and that I've licked this polio infection? I've been here a lot longer than Abigail. When will I be transferred to the… the… transition wing?"

Frank and Ernie looked at each other. A look of consternation clouded their faces. Finally, Frank offered a weak response, "Well, Miltie, you're just going to have to ask Dr. Frederick that question. We simply don't know, but even if we did, you would still need to talk it over with him."

Milton's spirits had temporarily lifted with the thought of getting out of his iron lung and returning to normal life. But Frank's lackluster, evasive response popped that balloon, and he settled back down dejectedly, dreading the possibility that he might never escape his iron prison. In truth, he admitted to himself that he simply didn't feel like he was getting any better. He still had frequent bouts with coughing up phlegm, and he realized that, in spite of the physical therapy exercises he was doing, his body was getting weaker confined as it was within his iron prison.

From the moment he met Abigail, he knew that she hadn't been as sick as he was and that she might be just a "short-timer" here in the iron lung ward, like several other patients who came and went after just a short stay. However, there were several other patients in the ward who had been here when he first arrived who were still here, and he guessed that his condition consigned him to the same, long-term patient group.

Chapter Five

And so, Milton's life settled down into a boring repetition of day-after-day struggles for breathing air and just staying alive. Without a clock on the wall, he couldn't keep track of time. And without a calendar, he couldn't really keep track of the passage of the days either. His days were all alike. His new orderlies were likeable enough, but they were more stiff and formal than Jack or Sam. But, just the same, they came when he summoned them with the red button to help him with doing his business and cleanup afterwards.

Then one day, Milton dozed off for an afternoon nap. He was awakened by the sound of a familiar voice calling his name. "Good afternoon, Sleepyhead. Wake up and say hello."

Milton groggily came to full consciousness and realized it was Abigail's voice that he had heard. He raised his head and looked around to discover where the voice had come from.

It was indeed Abigail, standing there beside his iron lung... a great big smile spread across her face. "I've missed you so much, Miltie! How are you doing?"

"I... uh... I guess that I'm okay, Abigail. Same old routine... you know. But... you're back... and you're walking. You're all better! That's terrific!" Milton couldn't suppress his excitement at seeing his beloved Abigail standing there at his bedside.

"Not exactly, Miltie. I can only stand for minutes at a time, but then when I get tired, I have to sit back down again… like right now."

Abigail grasped the sides of a wheelchair that Milton hadn't seen and slowly lowered her petite frame back into the chair. "Whew, that's much better! It still hurts way too much to stand and walk."

Then, Miltie noticed that not only was Abigail in a wheelchair, but both her legs were encased in metal support braces.

Abigail started to tear up, and Milton felt momentarily guilty for making her cry. Milton backpedaled… "I'm so sorry Abigail… I didn't know. I thought for a moment that you were all healed and done with this polio nightmare. I didn't mean to make you cry."

"You didn't make me cry, Miltie," she sniffled. "I'm just so happy to be back here to see you again. When my father got word of the positive tests they were running on me and the likelihood that I had reached the point that I no longer needed to depend on the iron lung, he rushed over to the clinic that very evening, and requested my immediate release… in the dark of night. You were already asleep, and I didn't get to say goodbye to you. It was devastating and I cried for days."

Milton noticed a tall man in a dark blue suit standing behind Abigail's wheelchair in the shadow. He had at first surmised that it was another doctor, but when the man started squirming with Abigail's tears, he recognized that it was Abigail's father who had visited her so often during her internment in the clinic.

Abigail continued talking through her tears, "My father has something to say to you, Miltie. Daddy, please come around to where he can clearly see you."

The tall man stepped to the side of Abigail's wheelchair, and moved into Milton's field of vision. He started talking slowly, "I'm afraid that I owe you a big apology, young man. When I received word that Abigail could be released from the clinic, I couldn't wait to get her home again and hurried over to get the process moving. I'm afraid that I didn't give her adequate time to prepare to leave and to say her goodbyes. It was my fault, and I am so sorry if my actions caused you pain."

"Thank you, sir. I appreciate it."

"I want you to know, Miltie, how much I appreciate you being Abigail's friend here at the clinic. From what she tells me, you have added a ray of sunshine into her life again, a special joy I haven't seen in her eyes since her mother died. I have promised Abigail that I will drive her over here to the clinic every week so that she can visit with you. It would never do to abruptly break up friendships as precious as yours."

And Abigail's father kept that promise. Every weekend he brought Abigail to the clinic to visit with Milton for a couple of hours. Abigail brought books she was reading and read to Milton so they could enjoy them together. One favorite that they both enjoyed very much was *Forfeit*, a pulp fiction novel by mystery writer Dick Francis. The book's background storyline was about the young wife of the novel's protagonist, James Tyrone, who contracted polio and had to live in a respirator canister… an iron lung. The novel's storyline resonated with both of them and brought them closer together.

They found out that Dick Francis' wife had in reality contracted the polio disease early in their marriage and had to live for a period of time in an iron lung. But she eventually recovered sufficiently to leave the canister behind and live an active life, even earning her pilot's license to fly. That fact gave them both hope for a brighter and more fulfilling future.

It was a great blessing for Milton just to have Abigail nearby and experience the adventure of visiting places in the world that their physical disabilities would otherwise never have allowed them to explore first hand. And without realizing it, Milton slowly fell in love with Abigail, a deep and abiding affection that would last forever.

Chapter Six

Over time, Milton gradually accepted the probability that he might never recover sufficiently to leave the iron lung and the polio clinic behind. His diaphragm and rib muscles weren't totally paralyzed, but the disease had left them greatly weakened. It appeared that, unless his physical therapy helped Milton to strengthen those breathing muscles so that he could breathe without the mechanical assistance from the iron lung, he might have to spend the rest of his life imprisoned in the metal canister that was keeping him alive.

But then fate took a turn for the better.

One morning as Milton was performing his morning constitutional with his orderlies, Dr. Frederick entered the bay and stood there in the entryway until the orderlies had finished their work. Then, he walked over to the side of Milton's canister and greeted him with a cheery smile.

"Good morning, Miltie. How are you doing today?"

"I'm okay, Dr. Frederick, a little bored out of my mind with just lying here. I could use a little exercise."

"Well then, I've got some pretty good news for you. You've been selected to try out a new technology for polio patients. It's still very much in the experimental stages at this point, but its development has reached the stage where it needs to be tested by real-life polio patients. It's called a cuirass negative pressure ventilator."

"What's a c… c… cuirass? I've never heard that word before."

"Good question, Miltie. Back in medieval days, a cuirass was a piece of body armor made of metal or thick leather consisting of a breastplate and backplate fastened together to protect knights and conquistadors against being shot up and cut down by arrows, swords, and spears. Because of its similarity in appearance and function, the term 'cuirass' today denotes a ventilator which encloses the body in a hard-shell shield, leaving the arms free, which forces air in and out of the lungs by changes in pressure."

"Sounds intriguing, but does it work?"

"That's a question that we're looking to have you help us with, Miltie. It's a little like wearing an oversized, stiff-walled, wrap-around girdle, but it has the possibility to allow the polio patient to exit the iron lung and move around outside. So far, the bellows and battery for the contraption are a little bulky and so the patient can only move around with the assistance of a specially-adapted wheelchair with the battery and bellows attached. But it allows the patient to leave the iron lung for a period of time during the day. At night, patients can return to the iron lung for a more restful sleep. Sound like something you would like to try? Would you like to be one of the first test subjects to give the new technology a test drive?"

Milton was so excited that his voice fairly exploded on his next breathing cycle. "Yes, sir! Count me in! I want to be one of the first! How does it work?"

"It's really quite simple," Doctor Frederick responded. "Like a medieval cuirass, it's a hard-shell structure that is custom-fitted to the patient's body which creates a ventilation chamber right there on the chest area. It has a soft gasket around the edges to ensure patient comfort and preclude compression leaks and air escaping."

"How is it custom-fitted?"

"While the patient is wearing a special face mask to keep breathing going during the design process, fabricator technicians cover the patient's chest area with a special plaster composite material that quickly firms up making a mold of the patient's chest area to make the custom-fitted cuirass to size. Once they use the mold to cast the cuirass frame in metal, they wrap a gasket around the outside edges to make sure that it won't irritate the patient's skin, and then attach the tubes and wires to activate the equipment, much like it works in the iron lungs... only it's all greatly miniaturized... and it only covers the chest area."

"That sound's great! When can I get started?"

"I was hoping you would say that. How about right now, Miltie? I've got the fabrication technicians standing by in the foyer to come in with the plaster casting equipment to get the ball rolling. Frank and Ernie are ready to fit you out with a special positive pressure head apparatus mask called a CPAP to continue assisting your breathing in a limited way while the plaster cast dries. The fabrication team should have a custom-fitted hard-shell cuirass ready for you to try out by the end of the week."

Milton was beside himself with the anticipation of wearing the new cuirass when the technicians arrived with it to show him how to put it on. Once the straps around his back were in place, and they had checked the seal around the cuirass next to Milton's skin, the technicians opened the front doors of the iron lung and slid the cookie tray out with Milton still lying on it. They quickly hooked up the cuirass to the configuration of battery and bellows on the wheelchair and activated the system. Milton was elated that he could still breathe with the assisted breathing of the cuirass. Frank and Ernie took over from there. They assisted Milton with getting down off the cookie tray and lowering himself onto the special wheelchair. Then, once assured that the cuirass was still doing its breathing-assistance job, they wheeled Milton around the bay, up and down the rows of canisters.

Then, they moved away from the wheelchair and invited Milton to use the large chair wheels to move and steer it himself. His arm muscles were very weak, and that presented a bit of a chore for him, but he was successful in maneuvering the chair all the way down to the double doors at the end of the bay, turn it around, and steer it back to the side of his own canister.

When he got back around to the front of the iron lung next to the cookie tray, Dr. Frederick walked in and came down to where Milton sat enthralled with his new-found freedom.

"So, how's it going Miltie? Is the cuirass working okay for you? Are you getting sufficient breathing assistance to get all the air you require?"

"Yes sir. It's working just fine. And I can move around without the iron lung lugging me down. This is a great invention!"

"That it is, Miltie. What did you think of the positive pressure CPAP device that our orderlies put over your face to keep you breathing while the fabrication techs smeared the plaster cast mixture all over your chest? Did the CPAP do its job? It moves air in and out of your lungs in an exact opposite way of the negative pressure operation of the iron lung. They are doing experiments with devices like the CPAP in some labs to provide positive pressure full time."

"It seemed to do okay although not as well as the iron lung. It took a little getting used to and I struggled with it getting enough air to be comfortable."

"That's about what I expected. They have found that to make positive pressure devices work for polio patients for long term use, they have to stick a breathing tube of some sort down the patient's throat, or in some cases, cut a tracheostomy slit in the patient's neck to insert a breathing tube directly through to the lungs."

Milton grimaced as he considered that last option. He was comfortable enough sitting there in his wheelchair with the negative pressure breathing assistance of the cuirass without anyone having to cut a hole in his neck.

As Dr. Frederick turned to leave, Abigail and her father burst into the bay. Abigail moved as fast as she was able to manipulate the wheels of her wheelchair down to where Milton sat. She sidled up to him and held out her hands to greet him. "Congratulations, Miltie! You're mobile now. That's terrific! Can you breathe okay with that shell thing over your chest?"

"It's called a cuirass, Abigail... and yes, I can breathe just fine with it."

"You've broken free from the iron lung. You're no longer like the man in the iron mask that we read about in the Alexander Dumas novel,"

Abigail said all giggly. She paused to catch her breath, and then added softly, "I've waited so long just to hold your hand."

Mr. Drexel smiled as he realized that Abigail, his only daughter, was falling in love with Milton, and was grateful for the added joy that it brought into her life.

Milton looked in surprise at Abigail's happy, smiling, face... and blushed. He too had been dreaming about this moment for a long time coming, and now he couldn't think of anything appropriate to say, except, "Me too." He was absolutely tongue-tied. With all the people standing around watching them, he was at a loss for words, something profound to say to express his deepfelt feelings he had for Abigail.

Abigail's father stepped forward, "You know, young man, you've taken a giant step in your recovery this morning. When you are ready, I would like to invite you to come and live at our house. We've outfitted special rooms with the latest design in iron lungs for you and Abigail to rest in when you need it, and I've contracted medical support personnel to service your needs. What do you say? Would you like to leave the polio clinic behind and come live with us?"

Abigail's father's suggestion took Milton totally by surprise. He had been there at the clinic for what he estimated had been a couple of years now. He couldn't quite fathom what that kind of change in his life this would be. He looked over at Dr. Frederick who smiled and nodded his head in approval.

"Our job here at the clinic is to help polio patients recover sufficiently so that they are able to return to their homes and continue their lives. Unfortunately, with both your parents gone now, you don't have a home to go to. Mr. Drexel's kind offer sounds to me like just the ticket. You can leave here anytime you say you are ready."

"Did you hear that, Miltie?" Abigail gushed. "You can leave here anytime you are ready, and come home and live with us. Would you like that? I hope so!"

Things were moving very fast for Milton and his head was spinning. "Well, yes! I would like that a lot!"

Milton leaned over to shake Mr. Drexel's hand, but he leaned a bit too far and lost his balance because of the added weight of the cuirass. He fell forward out of the wheelchair, hitting his head on the hard linoleum-covered floor. He passed out, losing full consciousness. When he awakened, he was back in his iron lung and the attending physician was running tests to see if he had been ill-affected by the fall.

"It seems to me, young man, that you were extremely lucky. You're alert and tracking my finger in front of your face well. I don't detect any problems with your mental acuity, and I don't detect any broken bones or abrasions. You should be back on your feet shortly, but I advise you to be more careful when you're out and about wearing the cuirass."

Chapter Seven

Life in the Drexel Mansion exceeded Milton's wildest expectation. He and Abigail had private rooms outfitted with the latest in iron lung technology. Although Abigail didn't have any immediate need for the iron lung, it was there available for her to retreat to for a rest in case of a breathing emergency. The enormous mansion had elevators connecting every floor and emergency backup generators in case of power failure.

Mr. Drexel had construction workers rebuild portions of the east wing of the mansion adding an extensive library of popular and classical books, an exercise room loaded with high-tech exercise and physical therapy equipment, a sauna and a steam room, a whirlpool bath, an exercise swimming pool, a conservatory music room, and a home movie theater with plush seating and a 16-mm projector.

Mr. Drexel worked a deal with a movie distribution firm to rent movies in the 16-mm reel format and had one of the house servants trained to operate the equipment. Every Friday evening was movie night in the Drexel mansion for Abigail, Milton, and all of the house servants. Mr. Drexel frequently freed up his busy schedule to join them. One of the plush theater chairs even had hook-ups for Milton's cuirass equipment so that he could transfer from his wheel chair setup to a more comfortable perch from which to watch the movies.

Mr. Drexel had physical therapists come to the house three times a week to work out with Abigail and Milton, helping them with exercises to strengthen their breathing and arm and leg muscles. Gradually, over time, they managed to achieve great progress and Abigail didn't need to use the leg braces any more. Milton grew strong enough to be able to switch back and forth himself without any assistance from his iron lung which he used to sleep in at night, and his cuirass-mounted wheel chair that he used to get around during the day.

One of the special perks that Abigail's father set up for Abigail and Milton was an educational degree program. Mr. Drexel was a big financial contributor to a local university, and he found them more than willing to free up professors' time to administer classes in the Drexel Mansion in their subject specialties so that Abigail and Milton could pursue academic degrees. Abigail was more interested in the biological sciences, and Milton was drawn to mechanical and electrical engineering. With the passage of the years, they both completed bachelor's degrees, then master's degrees, and finally doctorates in their areas of specialization. They also realized just how much they loved and depended upon each other.

The physical therapy that Abigail and Milton engaged in produced big dividends. As his musculature strengthened and matured, he had to have several additional fittings for his cuirass so that they comfortably fit his chest area and provided a good seal to prevent leakages.

More importantly, as Milton's diaphragm muscles strengthened, he was able to wean himself from the mechanical assist of the iron lung and the cuirass to the point that he could breathe quite effectively without the assistance of either. He still found it necessary to wear leg braces, and he used a cane to avoid losing his balance and falling. Abigail improved to the point that she no longer had to rely on her wheelchair to get around, and she didn't need to use the leg braces either.

One Sunday evening, Abigail and Milton were sitting around the dining room table with her father, Mr. Drexel, who was very interested in the post-doctoral projects that Abigail and Milton were engaged in. The dinner conversation bounced back and forth between topics on biology and mechanical engineering. Abigail's and Milton's research interests had converged, and they found common ground working on a project to perfect CPAP technology for breathing assistance for patients with obstructive sleep apnea and chronic obstructive pulmonary disease.

Positive pressure ventilation technology had passed through the early exploratory phase way back in the 1930s, but CPAP research had been given an enormous boost during the polio epidemic in the 1950s. The technology had advanced a great deal since Milton had used a primitive CPAP apparatus to breath while the technicians had covered his chest with plaster cast material to manufacture his first form-fitting cuirass. In recent years, CPAP equipment was fast becoming the treatment of choice for sleep apnea patients.

While Milton's research interests focused on the mechanically-assisted facets of breathing and walking, Abigail's interests focused on the physiological aspects of the challenges suffered by patients afflicted with the polio virus. Her research revealed that most polio patients with impaired respiration muscles and diaphragm, were able to move about freely from the confines of their iron lungs for limited amounts of time before they had to return to the canisters for rest and recuperation. Most suffered some degree of sarcopenia, a condition characterized by skeletal muscle mass atrophy. Such disuse atrophy was usually found to be reversible, but it typically required a significant amount of physical exercise therapy over an extended period of time. Exercise and a healthy diet were critical to the recovery, but even with that, recovery from muscular atrophy was a slow process.

As Abigail and Milton discussed their research work, Abigail laughed and remarked, "Oh, Dad, we didn't mean to bore you with all of the details of our post-graduate research. It's pretty dull stuff to most folks."

"Actually, honey, I'm extremely interested about all of the tedious details you've been bouncing around, personally and professionally."

"What do you mean by professionally? How does this all fit in to what Drexel Industries is involved in?"

"Good question, Abigail. Give me a minute or two to clear the house so that we can talk about it comfortably here around the table."

Mr. Drexel rang a little bell to the side of his plate to summon his butler. When he appeared, Mr. Drexel gave him terse instructions: "William, I want you to go throughout the house and dismiss all of the staff. Give all of the servants the rest of the day off. Tell them to stop doing whatever they are working on right now. They can pick up on it tomorrow at the beginning of a new day. Please come back when you have assured that everyone is out of the house and all doors and windows are secured."

As the butler left the room to carry out his instructions, Mr. Drexel turned back to face Abigail and Milton. "This shouldn't take too long. What we have to discuss now to answer your question is for your ears only… highly classified, national security stuff."

Milton was taken by surprise by all the precautions against anyone else becoming privy to what he had considered trivial postprandial dinner conversation.

William returned fifteen minutes later to report that the house was now empty and all the house staff had departed.

"That was pretty fast, William." Mr. Drexel commented. "How did you get them moving so fast?"

"Oh, I just reached into my pocket for the household mad money and gave everyone a hundred-dollar bill to hurry over to the mall and buy something special for themselves. They practically stampeded for the door."

"That was smart thinking William. So now, will you please join us here at the table. We have much to be talking about."

Abigail and Milton looked back and forth from Mr. Drexel and William in surprise that the butler now had a seat at the table. Abigail stammered, "D…D… Dad, do you mind telling us what is going on here?"

Chapter Eight

Mr. Drexel just smiled knowingly as he looked around the table, eyeing everyone in the room. He cleared his voice and said, "Perhaps we should begin with introductions." Motioning to William, he continued, "Abigail… Milton… I would like you to meet William T. Atherton, Ph.D. Dr. Atherton is one of the country's leading astrophysicists, specializing in cosmogeny and extraterrestrial life. I met Dr. Atherton at a conference last year, and we became engaged in discussing his research interests… the possibility of life on other planets in other galaxies in the cosmos. I invited Dr. Atherton to come live here in the mansion to be able to conduct his research away from prying eyes."

"Wow, that's impressive!" Milton managed to sputter with no attempt to disguise his astonishment and admiration. Dr. Atherton was a very youngish looking man, probably still in his early twenties… quite an accomplishment for one so young, he thought.

Mr. Drexel noted Milton's outburst response and continued without breaking stride. "Dr. Atherton has been working on a series of NASA and DOD sponsored projects. Most of them are black projects, and I'm not at liberty to discuss any details. However, Dr. Atherton is working on a project near and dear to the work of Drexel Industries. He's a strong proponent for the plurality of worlds and life on other planets, and he's helping us to develop a space colonization project for a planet many light years away from good old Mother Earth."

"What planet is that, Daddy? How far away is it?"

"It's one of several planets in orbit around a star we call Kepler 452. Kepler is a star system that's a little over 1400 light years away."

"Why select a star system that's so far away? Aren't there any closer that would do?"

"Not that we know about yet. Kepler 452b is a planet in that star system, slightly larger than planet Earth, and appears to be the only planet in the system that we can confirm lies in the Goldilocks zone."

"What's the Goldilocks zone, Mr. Drexel?" Milton asked.

Mr. Drexel chuckled. "I'm going to ask William to field that one. That's his area of expertise."

Dr. Atherton smiled and responded, "The Goldilocks zone is the positioning of a planet in orbit around a star where it is neither too hot nor too cold. Liquid water neither freezes nor steams away. In other words, it may be ideally located to support life as we know it. That factor alone makes it fairly unique for a planetary system in our near vicinity. If all other factors line up, it just may prove to be a habitable alternative to Earth, where large portions of our human population could emigrate one day should it ever become necessary."

"Why would it ever become necessary to leave Earth and colonize Kepler 452b?" Abigail asked, puzzled.

"Well," Dr. Atherton responded, "there are all kinds of possibilities that could render our home planet here uninhabitable… prolonged solar flares and solar storms, global nuclear war, super volcano eruptions, massive earthquakes, shifts in plate tectonics and polar reversals, tsunamis, and even the potential for a wayward comet or asteroid crashing into Earth and throwing us into nuclear winter. Life here on Earth is really positioned in a delicate balance, and any one of those factors could possibly change life for us almost overnight."

Milton was quick on the uptake, "If this colonization project is so top secret and hush-hush, just why are you sharing all of this information with us?"

Mr. Drexel laughed. "I can tell you are already one step ahead of me. I've attempted to steer somewhat your educational journey thus far. The two of you have been studying for years developing a solid background in just the kinds of expertise I can put to work on the development of the space colonization project that is already well underway. I would like the two of you to become integrally involved in the research and implementation phase of multiple subprojects to prepare an operational intergalactic vehicle... an ark... to transport a pilot group of scientists, engineers, and colonists to Kepler."

"That's it?"

"Oh, there's much more," Mr. Drexel said. "Your joint background experience with overcoming the effects of the polio virus and living in iron lungs for an extended time in your early life will be invaluable for helping our engineers design cryogenic sleep chambers for the long trip to Kepler. From your practical experience surviving in iron lungs, you will be able to offer up practical insights that the experts would probably miss in the short run."

Milton and Abigail were clearly intrigued by the whole idea of working on such a grandiose project. "When do you want us to get started, Daddy?" Abigail asked.

"Well now, that's the primary reason for this conversation around the dinner table. William will be departing for his work assignment lab area in two days. I would like you both to prepare to hitch a ride with him to accompany him on the journey."

"Journey! What do you mean?" Milton asked. "Just where is the project research center located?

"I think you'll be intrigued by the answer to that question. The project is already well underway with the construction of the superstructure of a huge intergalactic space vehicle on the far side of the moon."

"The far side of the moon... but, why there?"

"The moon's rotation is such that it always shows one side toward Earth and the other side always away from earth. In other words, the far side of the moon is a perfect hiding spot to construct such a large space vessel without being detected. That should allow us to keep the project secret until we get closer to launch time. My engineers have been hard at work on the craft for several years now. The basic exterior framework has already been completed, but much work remains to be accomplished on the interior design. That's where you come in."

Mr. Drexel looked back and forth from Abigail to Milton and smiled reassuringly. "Are you up for the challenge? Does this sound like something you would like to have a major role in?"

Chapter Nine

It was a flurry of activity for Milton and Abigail during the next few days packing their clothes and other gear for the trip with Dr. Atherton. When the time came to depart, Mr. Drexel gathered the team together in the mansion dining room and gave both Abigail and Milton a loving hug.

"I won't be going with you just yet, but I'll try to join you before too long. When you get to your new work labs, jump in and make a difference. You won't be in charge of anything, but you will have an advisory role on any subproject where you think you can make a difference. I'll be looking forward to reading your reports."

As they took the elevator down to the ground floor, a long, sleek limousine with darkened windows pulled up in front of the house. The chauffer assisted his passengers in loading up their luggage and then moved the sleek machine away from the house and into the urban traffic pattern. He drove for several hours out of town and into the countryside until they approached an imposing fence line with an automatic sliding access gate into what appeared to be a vast estate property. The chauffer slowed down sufficiently to key a password into the dashboard computer and then drove by as the gate slid open and then closed behind them.

They drove another few miles along a paved country road until the driver brought the limo to an abrupt halt in front of a large hanger. The chauffer turned his head and said matter-of-factly, "This is where you get off. They'll be waiting for you inside to load up the helicopter." As they dismounted from the limousine, several men rushed out of the hanger and took their baggage to load into a large cargo helicopter and then assisted the group to load up and get strapped in. Milton observed that the crew loaded Abigail's and his iron lung equipment in the helicopter's huge storage bay.

The helicopter lifted off and flew for what seemed to Milton another several hours until it finally set down at an isolated launching site inside another high security fence in the middle of nowhere. The helicopter pilot advised them that they were many miles from any town, and the launch of their transport rocket wouldn't be observed by any prying eyes.

The launch crew helped the team to transfer their luggage to the transport rocket and then get dressed in pressurized suits with fishbowl helmets. As Milton and Abigail settled down into their seats, Atherton remarked, "It appears that your father has quite an operation going here. I'll bet that the security is so good that no one is aware of what is happening on the far side of the moon."

"I think you're probably right," Abigail responded with a giggle. Isn't it exciting! I've been meaning to ask again, just why is it necessary to build this interstellar craft on the far side of the moon? What's the significance of that anyway? Would you please explain it all again."

"Sure, Abigail," Atherton replied. "The moon's rotational pattern is such that it always has one side faced toward Earth and the other side faced away. Thus, the construction site for this interstellar craft that we're building will go unobserved from any Earth-bound observatories or telescopes. The mass of the moon will simply obfuscate any unneeded and unwanted observation."

While they were talking, a member of the flight crew checked out their suits and remarked, "You won't be needing the helmets for quite a while just yet. Park them on the bench beside you until I give you the word to put them on. Meanwhile, I need you all to take this pill. It will help you with the sudden acceleration and G force as we lift off. Nothing to worry about, but some people have been known to pass out."

"What kind of pill is it?" Abigail asked.

"Well, ma'am, it's a little like Dramamine on steroids. It will relax you and help you avoid potential motion sickness. It might even help you sleep through the majority of the flight."

Milton, Abigail, and Mr. Atherton all promptly complied and took the paper cup of water that the crew member dispensed to them, but waited to swallow the pill.

The captain of the rocket ship came by for a quick chat with his passengers to reassure them about the journey they were about to undertake. "Howdy, folks. My name is Captain Bill Rothwell. I'm the commander for this shuttle. It's my job to get you safely to the far side of the moon. We'll wait about thirty minutes for the meds to take effect, and then we'll give you a countdown warning to prepare you for the launch. The trip to the far side of the moon actually goes pretty fast overall. We're using some new technology that we acquired by reverse engineering some extraterrestrial equipment we acquired from a UFO crash site in Mexico."

"What's a UFO?" Abigail asked.

Captain Rothwell responded. "Most people today just refer to them as flying saucers. The term UFO stands for Unidentified Flying Object and is quickly coming into common usage, particularly in official US government channels. A rather large UFO crashed down a couple of hundred miles south of the border in Mexico. The Mexican government was very cooperative and more than a little anxious to get all of the alien crash wreckage off their hands. We've had it for several years now, and we gleaned quite a bit of high-tech information to advance our rocket science. New stuff... never been used before here on Earth. We've run some test flights with it during the past six months, and it performs well... perhaps better than expectations. I can't wait to see how it works on our bird for our maiden flight with it to the moon. It used to take us several days to get there. Now the project engineers are projecting that we'll get there in just over one day. Quite a feat for travelling 239,000 miles."

Milton, Abigail, and Dr. Atherton swallowed their pills and then settled back in their padded seats. Abigail quickly responded to the sedative medication and was asleep even before the liftoff countdown.

The liftoff was uneventful from Milton's perspective. The excessive G force was spread out over the first several minutes of the flight, and then it diminished to nothing as the shuttle transport rocket cleared Earth's gravitational pull and continued on into space. Looking through the passenger observation porthole, everything went black, like someone had turned the lights out. At the same time, millions of dots of light came into view, evidence of the myriad galaxies and star systems whose light was sufficient to illuminate the blackness of space that enveloped them. Milton and Dr. Atherton continued staring out the porthole and discussing the immensity of the cosmos for a few minutes and then both of them reluctantly succumbed to the sedative and drifted off to sleep.

Chapter 10

Milton slowly awakened to the sensation of someone shaking him gently on the shoulder. He slowly opened his eyes and realized it was the flight crewmember who had administered the sedative to them for the long flight to the moon.

"Are we there already?" Milton asked optimistically. "Seems like I just dozed off."

"Yes... the sedative pill has that effect. You've been out cold for the whole day. You'll be shaking off its effects for the next several hours."

Milton's conversation with the shuttle rocket crewman awakened Abigail and Dr. Atherton. Like Milton, they yawned deeply and stretched their arms over their heads. It was a slow recovery process.

The crewman prompted them to put on their fishbowl oxygen helmets as a precautionary measure as they transferred from the transport shuttle through the airlock to the lunar base.

The Commander of the base was there to greet them as they disembarked.

"Welcome to Lunar Base Armstrong. I'm Captain Joshua Parker. I hope that your flight aboard the Terra Luna Express was an enjoyable experience. You'll notice that we saved budget money on refreshments during the flight by having you sleep all the way through it. But fear not, we're going to rectify that right now in the command briefing room. Please follow me. We'll take care of formal introductions in just a minute."

Captain Parker led them down a long passageway to a large briefing room with chairs set up in a semicircle around a plain white wall. As they walked through the corridors, Milton spied a large electronic safety sign posted on a bulkhead wall just outside the conference room.

The sign. simply said:

97 DAYS SINCE THE LAST ACCIDENT OR INJURY
ON THE ARK CONTRUCTION SITE.

0 DAYS SINCE THE LAST ACCIDENT OR INJURY
DURING BASE OPERATIONS.

Milton turned to Captain Parker and commented, "0 days since the last accident. I hope that no one was seriously injured in the incident."

"Oh no. Not at all. One of our enterprising young ensigns was experimenting with his invention of microwave popcorn, and he accidently got his hand in contact with a blob of red-hot molten butter. His hand will heal up in a week, but it's a good lesson for us all to know our materials and avoid getting into situations where someone might get hurt."

"I don't have a clue of what you are talking about, but you can bet that I'm going to run that one to the ground. I love popcorn."

As Milton, Abigail, and Dr. Atherton sat down in the command conference room, a server brought in plates and trays of hors d'oeuvres and petite sandwiches. Motioning to the trays, Captain Parker quipped: "Please help yourselves. You are probably hungrier than you think. Your baseline hunger indicator will be pegged after just a few minutes here on the lunar base. You deserve more than simple finger food, but I need to point out that everything on the serving tray was produced right here on the base. Meanwhile, I would like to get introductions taken care of."

"Again, I'm Captain Joshua Parker. I've been responsible for the establishment and development of Lunar Base Armstrong. I am an officer in the budding U.S. Space Corps, offspring of the U.S. Air Force."

Milton interrupted at that point, "Excuse me, sir, but I wasn't aware that we had a Space Corps. When did that happen?"

"We've been around for almost five years now. It's still all Top Secret... hush-hush." Pointing to a Space Corps patch on his sleeve, he continued with a sly grin, "And now that I've let the cat out of the bag, you'll have to consider killing yourselves."

The Base Commander laughed, obviously pleased with his expertly delivered, but well-worn joke.

"Ladies and gentlemen gathered around on the periphery, would you all step forward one by one in order. Introduce yourselves and explain what your duty position is and what you really do here on the lunar base."

One by one, each member of the crew gathered in the briefing room stepped forward and took care of their self-introductions. When they were finished, Dr. Atherton stood and spoke: "Thank you. It's good to see many of you again. I believe that I have met everyone Earthside or on a previous trip up here, and I believe you know me well. However, I would like for all of you to meet Miss Abigail Drexel and Mr. Milton Jeffries. You will all certainly recognize the name Drexel. Abigail is the daughter of our benefactor who is picking up the tab for this venture."

"Abigail and Milton have another claim to fame. They are both survivors of the polio virus and have been asked by Mr. Drexel to join our enterprise here because of their experience lying for extended periods of time in iron lung canisters, healing from the effects of the virus. According to Mr. Drexel, the idea is that they are probably as close as we can get to expertise on cryogenic sleep systems that we're having a challenging time developing here at the lunar base. Oh, and as an aside, it might have something to do with the fact that each has multiple Ph.Ds in several technical fields that will be of great utility to us as we confront the challenges and conundrums of building an interstellar ark to haul upwards of a thousand souls through the depths of space to a new star system many light years away. Mr. Drexel asked me to explain to you all that Milton and Abigail are here in a purely advisory role. They are not in the command structure and, although they may contribute ideas and suggestions, they are not in the decision-making role for the lunar base or the construction of the ark. Their positioning will allow them freedom of movement to float around the base and construction site to get a feel for what's going on and to make occasional observations and suggestions as appropriate."

With the introductions out of the way, Captain Parker motioned to the white wall at the front of the room. "Marv, please roll the video."

Milton was astounded to learn that the wall was actually an enormous video screen. It was at least four feet across. It was a far cry from the TV screens in common use back on Earth. He stood and walked around to the side of the oversized screen just to see how thick it was. He was shocked to see that it was impossibly thin, certainly not enough room for an array of vacuum tubes within.

Turning back to face Captain Parker, he asked, "How do you fit vacuum tubes in a screen as thin as this one, sir?"

Colonel Parker laughed, "It's not like an old-fashioned vacuum tube projection screen that you are probably used to. It's based on new microtechnology that they recently reverse-engineered from a downed alien spacecraft back on Earth. That's one of the first projects I would like you to take a look at to see how this new microtechnology could be used to control and pilot the ark space craft.

An attendant entered the briefing room with a small tray of cookies, advising them that they might benefit from eating a cookie or two following their flight to settle their stomachs. Abigail eagerly grabbed a couple of the cookies and scarfed them up. "I would sure like to see your kitchen facilities where you can whip up cookies as delicious as these."

"Oh, they weren't cooked in a kitchen facility," said the steward. "I cooked them in the break room in the microwave oven."

"Microwave oven! What's that?" Abigail asked bewildered.

"It's a new technology that we adapted from the radar systems that were used during the war. Our World War II radar technicians found that they could heat up their lunches by positioning them in the radar beam in front of their equipment. After the war, with the wholesale stand-down from the production of war materiel, an engineer found an ingenious use for the no-longer-needed radar technology. And voila... now we have what some folks are calling the 'radar range.' They're about to become quite popular back on Earth. Pretty neat technology!"

Milton chimed in, "And apparently, they can even pop popcorn in them. Now that's what I call a magnificent innovation! My hat is off to the young crewmember who risked life and limb to bring the radar range technology on line here at the lunar base. I hope that he heals up quickly."

Everyone in the briefing room had a good laugh about the popcorn as Captain Parker interrupted the conversation, inviting Abigail, Milton, and Dr. Atherton to reposition their chairs to form a semi-circle to face the big video screen. "I have a little surprise for you all... It's a personal greeting from Mr. Drexel to be shared upon your arrival here at the base."

The screen fluttered white momentarily, and then the image of Mr. Drexel appeared. "Hello all. I'm glad to see that you made it safely to your new home away from home. You've got a lot of important work to do. I'll soon make the journey there to join you when I can free up some of the details of my oversight work here on good ol' Terra Firma."

"What do you mean... glad to see us?" Milton asked. "Is this a two-way video hookup? You can see us and talk with us?"

"That's right, Miltie," Mr. Drexel chuckled.

"But how are you getting around the communication void here on the backside of the moon with it masking radio transmissions with the Earth."

"That was fairly easy to address. We just worked a deal with the Space Corps to set up a network of communication satellites so that we never lose line-of-sight contact with Earth-based systems."

"That would work. The two-way video hookup is pretty cool technology," Milton acknowledged. It will come in very handy for the long trip to Kepler 452b. I hope I get the opportunity to work with that system."

"And that you shall, my boy," Mr. Drexel responded. "But first, we have a personal matter to attend to... Fathers are in a habit of embarrassing their daughters incessantly, and, I'm no exception. Abigail, Milton spoke with me in private before your departure and asked for your hand in marriage, which I quickly acceded to. I can't imagine a better mate for my only daughter. But things got moving so fast that we didn't have time to address the issue on Earth. Abigail, you've spoken with me on numerous occasions about wanting to marry Milton one day. Are you still as eager as you were before liftoff to the moon?"

"Oh, yes, Daddy…more than ever."

"That's good… that's very good. Then we have everyone present we need to pull this off. I previously spoke with Captain Parker. As Base Commander he has agreed to officiate in the ceremony. He has the legal authority to conduct marriages, and I believe that he is ready to begin. Am I correct in that, sir?"

"Yes, sir, Mr. Drexel, I am absolutely ready. If my staff would please step forward and assemble yourselves in a larger semi-circle around the bride and groom. I believe that someone has prepared a veil and flowers for the bride. Dr. Atherton, would you please serve as best man and stand here to the side of Milton. I'll ask my second in command, Lieutenant Colonel Debra Baker, to please serve as Maid of Honor and stand here beside Abigail. There, I think that we can get started. Abigail, are you ready? Milton, are you ready?"

Abigail and Milton looked at each other with love in their eyes and Milton pulled her closer next to him.

"It appears so. Then let's get moving on the first formal wedding ceremony to take place on the moon. Mr. Drexel, are you ready to give the bride away? Abigail and Milton, if you would please join hands…"

At that point, Marv cued the recording of the bridal march and the Lunar Base Commander proceeded with the ceremony.

Chapter 11

At the conclusion of the wedding ceremony, the entire wedding party adjourned to a neighboring bay where an elaborate spread had been laid out, far in excess of the meager trays of hors d'oeuvres previously served. Another large video screen had been positioned at one end of the serving table, and the visage of Mr. Drexel dominated the room as he grinned with delight at the culmination of the marriage proceedings.

The crew from the transport rocket had been preparing their craft for the return trip and arrived at the reception slightly late, out of breath from running the full distance from the entry portal, still wearing their pressurized space suits and fish bowl helmets. Captain Rothwell, the shuttle commander, saw a great opportunity for a bridal reception gag moment. Taking a goblet from a tray on the table, he raised his glass high and proposed a toast.

Nodding to the couple, he announced jubilantly, "To the bride and groom, may you enjoy many years of adventure and love together."

Then he raised his goblet the rest of the way high in the air and then brought it down to the level of his face as if to drink. The goblet promptly shattered against his tempered fishbowl helmet. The whole thing took everyone by surprise and the whole bay erupted in raucous laughter. It was a great entree for getting into the spirit of the wedding feast laid out before them.

After several hours of celebrating and festivating, Captain Parker tapped a spoon on the side of his goblet and announced, "Well, folks, we've all had a great time this afternoon helping this young couple celebrate their nuptials. Now I propose that we all break away and return to our work stations so that I can escort Abigail and Milton to their honeymoon suite, which will become their permanent living quarters here on the lunar base for the duration."

Everyone clapped and cheered as the Base Commander led Abigail and Milton from the bay down a long passageway to a hatch doorway bedecked with ribbons and flowers. "I believe this must be it. I leave you to continue your celebrating in private. Many happy returns of the day."

With that, the Commander did a smart about face and walked away back down the passageway they had just traversed. Abigail and Milton turned back around to face the door and saw a little hand-lettered sign on a yellow Sticky Note posted on the edge of the portal next to a large round inset button. The sign simply said,

--PUSH HERE—

Not needing any further encouragement, Milton pushed the button and the hatch divided into three components as it slid open. As the couple passed through the hatchway into their honeymoon suite, the door slid back tightly together.

Chapter 12

When Milton and Abigail awoke after a long sleep period exacerbated by the souped-up Dramamine, they got cleaned up and dressed and then went to the door to find their way back to the central passageway. As the door opened, they found a young man standing patiently outside across the way waiting for them.

"Good morning to you both," he said with a big grin. "My name is Willy. I hope you had a good rest. You've got a big day ahead of you."

"What do you mean?" Abigail queried.

"Well, Ma'am, I've been assigned to escort you on a walk-around tour of the base. You're dressed just fine for most of the tour, but we'll need to retrieve your spacesuits and fish bowl helmets in case we decide to exit through the pressure doors and take a brief tour of the construction taking place outside right now."

As they started their walk down the passageway back toward the main conference briefing room, Abigail noticed that everyone seemed to be wearing color-coded T-Shirts. "What's the meaning of all the different colors people are wearing?" she asked.

Willy spoke right up and responded, "Hasn't anyone explained that to you yet? Let's drop by the Lunar Base Quartermaster Shop and Sutler Inn and get you outfitted appropriately for the day."

"That's quite a mouthful!" Abigail giggled.

"Boy, you're right about that," Willy responded. "Most folks just call it the Sutler or the Q&S. It keeps things simpler."

"While we're at keeping things simple," Milton countered, "please just call me Milton."

"And me Abigail. I would much rather work on a less formal basis if that doesn't violate the organizational culture already in place."

"It doesn't. Most of us have already reached the same conclusion. You're going to fit right in here."

"Okay, Willy, let's get back to my original question… why all the different colored shirts?"

"Well, I wasn't in on that decision. It was decided in one of the base council meetings. The colors of the shirts generally indicate peoples' work assignments here on the moon base and interstellar ark construction. For example, people whose work assignment is primarily here on the base wear blue shirts with a large A, for Armstrong, on the front. Black shirts are for folks who are construction engineers or colonists in some form or another, and the black is for the black of space. Some of the colonists have taken to include a graphic of their area of colonization specialty… like a cow for animal husbandry or a tree for forestry horticulture or a sheaf of wheat for domestic horticulture and food products, or a beehive for an apiarist."

Abigail was amused by the ingenuity of the base organizers. "We're going to be working on all aspects of base operations and ark construction, so what color would we need to get at the Q&S?"

"Oh, they have a special shirt for folks like you… a black and white vertical-striped shirt that makes you look like a referee for a sporting event."

Milton mused, "That's probably not a bad description for our role here for now."

After a short stop at the Q&S changing rooms, Milton and Abigail emerged back into the corridor wearing black and white referee shirts. They continued their walk down the passageway in the direction of the main briefing room where they found Captain Parker waiting for them with a modest breakfast buffet set up against the far wall.

"Good morning, folks. Good to see you today."

"Excuse me sir, all of the base's clocks seem to be set for the same time, but how do you know really whether it's morning or night."

"Good question, Abigail. It's all rather arbitrary, but with a caveat. Some people back on Earth refer to where we're located as the dark side of the moon. Nothing could be further from the truth. The moon rotates so that it always displays the same face towards Earth, that's true, but that doesn't make the other side here the 'Dark Side.' In fact, when the Sun is beating down on this side of the moon facing away from Earth, it can get oppressively hot with the sun's radiation. The variance between sunlight and shadow can result in enormous variations in temperature, from as hot as 260 degrees Fahrenheit in full sun to a minus 280 degrees when it's dark. That's one of the reasons why our construction workers who are working outside the confines of the base buildings, have to be extremely careful of direct sunlight or total shade. They all wear white uniforms and gloves and headgear and that tends to deflect much of the heat away from their bodies. Nevertheless, the construction schedule revolves around those times in between when the temperature is more manageable and not quite as dangerous."

"That brings up a question that has been bothering me," Milton said. "Where do you get your water to support an enormous operation like this? I would think that direct sunlight would have boiled away any surface water long ago."

"You're absolutely right, Milton. That's why the lunar base was established where we did. We are located close to a large crater with steep sides where the shadows from the sun never quite reach the bottom. When we performed our initial surveys of the moon, we discovered large quantities of water in the bottom of the deep craters. We only have to pump it out and purify it for potable water."

"But is there enough water to sustain base operations and the ark when we're ready to launch?"

"Actually, I'm told there's sufficient water many times over. It shouldn't prove a problem in the near future."

"And in the far future?"

"Still not a problem. We'll just have to pump water from more distant craters and shelter the pipes from the effects of extreme temperature swings."

As Captain Parker was explaining the base water supply system to Milton and Abigail, they served themselves from the breakfast buffet and sat around one end of the conference table eating. It suddenly occurred to Abigail that all the rest of the people working here on the far side of the moon also had to eat and she wondered where the food supplies all came from.

Waving her hand in the direction of the breakfast buffet layout, Abigail asked, "Please, Captain, could you please explain where you get bacon and eggs, hash browns, toast, and the like here at the base. This is delicious, but it seems like quite a stretch."

"Actually, Abigail, it's not. All of the food consumed here on the base is produced by the team that will one day populate the ark and eventually colonize Kepler 452b. They'll provide all the food needed during the flight, and then establish food chains on the new planet when they get there. This is good training for the food teams for now. They are learning as they go."

"But," interrupted Milton, "where do you get the eggs and bacon and other farm commodities?"

"Same answer, Milton. We actually have several animal husbandry teams at work here setting up feeding stalls and slaughter houses and processing facilities. We've also got several horticultural teams putting together seeds and seed crops for the trip and eventual colonization. For instance, Horticultural Team A, for the Andes and high-altitude crops, specializes in rhizomes. They've already assembled over a hundred varieties of potatoes for current consumption here on the lunar base and future cultivation on Kepler. Those teams are also getting good practice in preparing for the ark's departure. We won't run out of French fries."

Captain Parker paused from laughing at his own joke and suggested a new topic: "The moon once had an active vulcanism presence. There are still a few volcanos spaced around the moon's Earth-side with evidence of them having erupted as recently as 15 million years ago, but there is also the possibility of more recent eruption activity in our own time."

"Is the lunar base in any danger here of a volcanic eruption?" Abigail asked.

"No, Ma'am," Captain Parker responded, "but when the volcanoes were active millions of years ago here on the far side, they left a large number of interconnected lava tubes, like the kind we encounter in Hawaii today. Those lava tubes have become quite the tourist attraction there."

"Yes, we know," Milton said laughing. "We once took a short stroll through a lava tube when we accompanied Abigail's father on a business trip to Hawaii. They had strung a series of lights along the tube's ceiling, and so it was well-lit. But it was still quite a frightening experience for me! I guess that I got an industrial-strength case of claustrophobia."

Captain Parker nodded agreement. "I felt the same thing. The lava tubes here are a little more than I can deal with. We've brought in a team of spelunkers and tunnel diggers from Earthside who are engaged in DOD black projects there, and they've been exploring the tubes for about half a year now. But it's a slow process. They have to mark every tube they enter so they don't get disoriented and lost. And all of the tubes interconnect in some way or another. But the real kicker is that there are so many of them, and the tubes go on for miles and miles. We've never got to the end of most of them... until recently... Then it got real sticky."

"What happened recently?" Milton asked.

"Unless you want to take another stroll through an endless maze of lava tubes, it will probably be more comfortable for you and Abigail to just sit down here facing the video screen and look at the most recent video shots the spelunker team captured."

Milton and Abigail swiveled their chairs around to face the video screen, and Captain Parker spoke into the control telephone on the conference table behind them. "Run the last set of videos, Marv. Be ready to hit pause and slo-mo if we need it."

The video screen came alive and they saw the darkness of a lava tube illuminated by several powerful hand flashlights. All of a sudden, the lava tube opened up into a large void where the lights from the flashlights couldn't reach.

"What are we looking at here?" Milton asked.

"Just this past week, the spelunkers encountered a huge cavern several kilometers deep into the moon's crust. They spent the better part of a week exploring the front end of the cavern when they came upon evidence of former occupation. We are not the first!"

That comment sent shivers up and down Milton's and Abigail's spines. "Are you saying that the spelunker team found evidence of former human activity down there?" Abigail asked.

"Yes," Abigail, "but not precisely human. Keep your eyes on the vid screen. It gets better... or worse, depending on your point of view."

Several more spelunkers appeared on the vid screen carrying a large, powerful searchlight powered by a portable generator. They used the searchlight to scan the walls of the cavern closest to the spelunkers, and then panned out over the cavern.

It was hard to judge distances from the video display, but it appeared that there was a large built-up, artificial structure several hundred meters down the slope into the cavern. The structure appeared to be made of metal but it was unusual in that it had no straight lines and no ninety-degree corners. Everything about the structure was rounded and curved. A portion of the top of the structure had broken away leaving a clear view into the interior.

"Freeze the frame, Marv, and pan in slowly now."

Gradually, the interior of the structure enlarged as the video frame zoomed in. What they observed surprised Milton and gave him pause in a terrifying kind of way. In the center of the exposed interior chamber, they could see what appeared to be the remains of a large individual sitting in an enormous platform chair. Spaced around the outer wall of the chamber, there were additional individuals seated in less ostentatious seats all surrounded by what appeared to be high tech consoles with keyboards and monitor screens.

Abigail observed, "That looks like the wreckage for a movie set for a science fiction film Milton and I saw a couple of months ago."

"Well, looks can be deceiving but that's exactly what I thought when I first saw it. And strangely enough, it looks very similar to the blueprints the design team produced for the bridge control room that will be the heart of ark operations."

"What did you do then, Captain?" Milton asked, breathing heavily. "This must have knocked your socks off."

"Not far wrong... As soon as the spelunking team spied the interior of the structure, they called topside for a crypto-zoologist and crypto-paleontologist team and a retro-engineering team to enter the structure and figure out what we had found."

"After a quick, cursory inspection of the interior cabin, the conclusion of the joint teams was just about what we initially thought about the structure. It appeared to be the bridge command center of an enormous space ship."

"The crypto-geologist team started out analyzing the physical makeup of the giant individual sitting in the platform chair. Although the individual was seated, it appeared to be about 12 feet tall. It had six elongated digits for fingers on each hand and a double row of teeth set in an exposed jawline. There was a large metallic helmet hanging off the side of its head exposing an explosion of what was once curly red hair, but now was gray and covered with volcanic dust. All of the individuals sitting on the periphery of the chamber had similar physical characteristics. The team took several samples from the individuals and sent them up to the surface for analysis to see if we could tell just how old these creatures were."

"Have they got the results back from analysis yet?" Milton asked.

"Yes, I just got word back from our lab that the specimens are approximately 15 to 20 thousand years old. And the DNA test yielded a surprising finding... the creatures weren't what we would call little green men extraterrestrials. Their DNA makeup was 99 percent human. They were just really big ancient humans. Who knows what they were doing on the moon 15 to 20 thousand years ago?"

"I'm wondering how they got their spaceship down inside the moon in a lava tube cavern," Abigail offered. "Something doesn't add up here. There doesn't seem to be much damage to their ship from this angle."

"What more have we learned about the race of people who left this here?" Milton asked.

"I'm glad you asked," Dr. Atherton responded. "We crated up several of the best-preserved skeletons and prepared them to ship Earthside on the next shuttle returning to earth. I had several important scientists and medical specialists lined up to give them a complete once over, but the Smithsonian somehow got wind of it all, and the crates disappeared right off the dock where the shuttle offloaded them. The crates haven't reappeared, and the Smithsonian, true to form, has denied all knowledge of the caper. I doubt that we'll ever recover those skeletons in the near future."

"Well, that's a surprise!" Abigail acknowledged.

"It shouldn't be a surprise," Dr. Atherton explained. "It's been going on for a very long time. The Smithsonian apparently goes out of its way to shape history along the preconceived notions of the established science of the day. In practice historically, that hasn't left any room for an active examination of the evidence of giant beings with six digits on their hands and feet, double rows of teeth in their mouths, and flaming red hair."

"Are you saying that this has been going on in archeological digs in the United States for a long time?"

"That's exactly what I'm saying. When Horace Greeley said, 'Go West, young man,' the early pioneers practically tripped over giants' bones every step of the way across Ohio and the rest of the Midwest. Not to mention the giants' bones that were discovered much further west in a guano dig in Lovelock Cave in Nevada. The Smithsonian and other museum authorities have spent decades undermining the reports of these discoveries and hiding or destroying the physical evidence. The bodies discovered here on the moon in the lava tube cavern corroborates those misrepresented histories, but it appears that the Smithsonian has already begun its work of historical obfuscation."

"Let's approach this discovery from a different tack," Milton suggested. "What did the engineers learn so far from all the technology in the chamber."

"Oh, I think we've just begun to scratch the surface. We are moving all of the transportable technology through the tubes to the surface to the reverse-engineering labs at the lunar base, and we'll have to access the rest in situ that can't be removed from the vessel. Our initial effort is just trying to figure out the technology's purpose and how it works. The main focus of our efforts right now is to figure out how the massive ship was powered. The spelunker teams haven't located any nuclear power sources so far, and there's no way that they could have carried sufficient liquid oxygen or liquid hydrogen or some other solid propellant to move the craft any great distance across the cosmos?"

"Sounds like we're off to a good start there," Milton observed. "I'm looking forward to working with the reverse-engineering and retrofitting teams soon."

Captain Parker laughed.

"Something else? Captain Parker?

"Well, yes. This is where it pays to be lucky more than smart. One of the engineers working to load up a large piece of technology on a pallet to take it up to the surface was dusting off a piece of alien equipment when he must have triggered some component that was still under power... live, active, and operational."

"What happened?" Milton asked inquisitively.

"The piece of equipment lifted off the floor and took flight. It went straight up into the air and rebounded off the ceiling of the chamber, and then clattered back to the floor. It was an antigravity device of some kind. We've got a lot of work to do trying to get ahead of the power curve to reverse-engineer all of the technology we've found in that chamber. If we can recover and figure out how most of it works, it could help us advance construction work on our ark by years, maybe decades."

"Did your teams discover anything else really exciting down there in the cavern?"

"Well actually, yes, and this is the best part."

"The best part?" Abigail asked.

"We initially thought that this was just a big space ship. But we augmented the spelunker team and they kept moving deeper into the vessel. Quite a bit deeper… 15 kilometers deeper. It is a long ship… a very long ship and it isn't just single level. There are at least twenty decks that they've explored so far. Our spelunkers teamed up with other teams already down there to see if they could assess the purpose of the vessel. On each of the twenty decks, they observed upwards of ten to twenty thousand compartments with platforms that they assumed were sleeping platforms."

"Why did they assume that they were sleeping platforms?" Abigail inquired.

"Because they were laid out in precisely the same pattern that we are constructing sleeping quarters in our ark. There just weren't any mattresses or pillows still extant after so many years. They have all disintegrated. And then there were the five to ten kilometers of animal stalls of all sizes, including what they think were enormous aquatic tanks for fish, porpoises, dolphins, small whales, and other sea creatures. No, all the teams looking into the question all concurred that it was an ark, similar to the one we have on the drawing boards, only much larger… much, much larger."

"How much larger?" Abigail asked.

"With compartmentalized components on each of the twenty decks running the length of the craft, this wasn't a mere exploratory vessel. It was a full-fledged, fully-staffed, and fully-stocked ark. They apparently were moving a significant portion of a planet's population."

"Are you sure?" Milton asked. "That would be an extraordinary coincidence for us to chance upon it right as we're building our own ark."

"Pretty sure. It removed all doubt when the spelunking team stumbled upon a huge section of the ship apparently designed as a repository for cow manure, bird guano, and other animal waste products. The spelunker who accidentally fell into the compartment over his head affirms that it was indeed manure and guano. Thousands of years of composting and decomposition hadn't taken the edge off the smell. He spent the next two days scrubbing down in hot soapy showers trying to lose the aroma, but it persists. For now, he eats alone in the dining facility."

Milton shuddered. "That sounds like one of my worst nightmares. Back on the farm where I grew up, my father maintained a manure pond to recycle cow and chicken manure as fertilizer for the next year's crop. But my father always cautioned me about getting too close to avoid the methane fumes that emanated from the pond. I'm guessing that the methane cocktail that the compartments once contained has long since dissipated."

"That's right, Milton. We quickly retrieved our crewman from the tank and started pumping oxygen into him. It turned out not to be necessary. When we took accurate measurements of the chemical composition of the air in that tank, it turned out not to be highly toxic and dangerous now."

"But to continue the story, Jack Tipton, our unfortunate manure tank diver couldn't get rid of the lingering smell from his experience. After two days of scrubbing down with vinegar and hot soapy water, you could still smell it. Tipton ended up using a month's supply of vinegar just trying to get rid of the stink. Bill Rothwell, the shuttle commander, tried to be helpful. He brought up several cases of commercial skunk odor neutralizer on his next trip up to the lunar base. Still, nothing quite did the job."

"So, what did Jack do? I can bet he was a social pariah until he got rid of the smell."

"That's right Milton. It was suggested that they partition off an entire wing of a new section of the ark just put into service to segregate the offensive odor from base personnel and construction workers."

"That seems pretty extreme."

"You had to smell it, Milton. Finally, Jack got fed up with the whole situation and bought out the Sutler's entire stock of Elsha, a men's cologne, and took a long soaking bath in it."

"Did that work?"

"Well, not quite. The Elsha pretty well masked the manure odor, but the residual aroma of the Elsha was overpowering, and the entire base crew voted to continue efforts to partition off Jack's section of the ark until he could get completely sanitized and odor free. That's probably going to take another month or so. I put Jack on paid leave at time-and-a-half pay to cover his misery, and he seemed somewhat satisfied with the resolution. Ah... the vicissitudes of life. They can sneak up on you when you least expect it."

Milton came back into their bedroom, exhausted from having traversed a good portion of the ark construction sites. He found Abigal sitting on the side of their bed, humming a nursery rhyme tune softly.

Milton laid his bubble helmet on his dresser as he entered the room. "What's with all the humming, Abigail?"

"It's a nursery rhyme that my mother used to sing to me before she died when I was just a little girl."

"Oh, it must have a special meaning for you."

"Oh, Milton, it does. Even more so now under our present circumstances."

Milton was puzzled. "What do you mean, Abigail? Why?"

"Do you remember the nursery rhyme, "Hey Diddle-Diddle?"

"Yes, I think so."

"Then sing it with me."

"Okay, I can do that, but you won't be particularly thrilled with my voice. I'm no singer. I can't carry a tune in a bucket."

"Oh, it's not your voice that I'm concerned with... it's the words. The words have a special meaning."

"Okay, if it makes you happy."

> Hey Diddle-Diddle, the cat and the fiddle,
> The cow jumped over the moon.
> The little dog laughed to see such sport
> And the dish ran away with the spoon.

"Thanks, Miltie,... Don't you see it?"

"See what?"

"Why the correlation to our being here on the lunar base building an ark?"

"How so? I'm a little vague on this one. I'm not much good with poetry. Help me out, please."

"Listen, silly. It's all metaphorical and symbolic. The cat is the caterpillar tractor earth movers that are all over the construction zone. The fiddle is the huge cranes that lift the steel girders into place. The cow jumping over the moon is the Taurus constellation... it just reflects how we keep seeing different angles of the constellations from here... same for the laughing little dog... that's the constellation Canis Minor. Finally, the dish and the spoon are the feedhorn focal points of our large dish telescope array."

"Don't you see.... It's all there. The rhyme is prophetic. It accounts for all the elements of our being here. Whoever penned the rhyme so long ago must have somehow looked into the future and saw what we are about here today."

"That seems a bit of a stretch to me, Abigail, but if it makes you happy, I'm all for it."

The correlation must have resonated with Milton more than he cared to admit because he went around all the next day humming the nursery rhyme tune stuck in his head.

Chapter 13

Milton, Abigail, Captain Parker, Dr. Atherton, and all of the team heads from both base operations and the ark construction crew were gathered around the conference table to discuss where they were on the construction schedule and other important issues.

Dr. Atherton kicked off the discussion. "Let's summarize what we have learned about Kepler 452b. Is it habitable? Beyond being located in the Goldilocks zone, does it meet all of the other planetary characteristics for colonization to support human life?"

Dr. Herb Beinhauser, lead scientist on the astrophysicist team, responded haltingly. "We have employed some of the most powerful telescopes available on earth focused on Kepler 452b, and they are even more effective here on the moon without having to look through all the layers of atmosphere from Earth. We have learned a great deal during the past two years. But it is a stretch to say that that we have confirmed all of the necessary planetary characteristics for colonization yet. There is only so much you can conjecture and predict with a powerful telescope from 1402 light years away. However, from what we have learned thus far, we believe that Kepler 452b will work out just fine, although we may need to do quite a bit of terraforming to make it entirely inhabitable for us once we arrive. The long pole in the tent is just getting there. Unless we can exploit some propulsion means to speed up the ark's acceleration and velocity getting there, we have a lengthy journey ahead of us that might amount to over a fourteen hundred years."

Dr. Atherton nodded his head in agreement, "When Mr. Drexel approached me years ago to enlist me in this formidable project, he acknowledged that the team engineers still didn't have the propulsion system for the ark figured out for the journey to Kepler 452b, but he was highly optimistic that we would work out a solution before long. Well, several years have since passed, and I don't believe that we are any closer today than we were back at the beginning. I believe that we have ignored the elephant in the room long enough. We simply must work out the details for the propulsion system or systems that will power the ark to Kepler 452b. For an interstellar flight there, in anything approximating a timely fashion, the devil is indeed in the details. The planet is approximately 1400 light years from Earth. Even if we were to rely on nuclear power to accelerate the ark to just below the speed of light, like Dr. Beinhauser rightfully pointed out, it would take upwards of a millennium and a half to get there. We simply must explore and implement more effective propulsion options for getting there more quickly, preferably within the life span of the original ark crew and the colonists who will hitch a ride on the ark."

Lane Stevenson, one of the project engineers, responded somewhat petulantly, "Agreed Dr. Atherton, we've looked at several possibilities… however, none of them help us to beat the time-acceleration speed limit."

Dr. Atherton smiled a weak grin. "I understand your frustration, Dr. Stevenson, but I think that there just might be some possibilities that we haven't thoroughly explored. The first would be passing through a nearby wormhole that would dump us out at the other end in the near vicinity of Kepler 452b. That's an option about which we know very little so far. We've discovered a number of black holes in our near vicinity but we haven't been able to put together a model that suggests that the ark and its passengers could survive such a passage."

Dr. Angus quickly added, "Nor do we have any idea how we could use a black hole to steer us in the direction of Kepler 452b. It wouldn't pay to fly 1400 light years and find that we had flown in the wrong direction."

Dr. Atherton nodded affirmation. "Well then, what are other options that might work?"

"Dr. Zinn, has your team made any progress with the propulsion issue?"

"Yes sir, as a matter of fact we have," responded Dr. Zinn, leader of the reverse engineering team. "Initially, we got overly focused on the antigravity aspects of the alien technology because it provided us so many solutions for bringing colonists and supplies up from Earthside to load the ark for the journey. It also provided us with a neat solution for overcoming all the physical challenges that we would otherwise face with muscle atrophy and bone deterioration, let alone overseeing the production of animal feed and meat and egg production for human consumption, during the long flight. Somehow, it slipped to the back burner that antigravity might just be the solution to all of our propulsion issues. Dr. Koroveshi's team recently ran some promising experiments that we think may pan out."

"Theoretically, however," Dr. Atherton pointed out, "gravity can't travel any faster than the speed of light either. At least, that's what the theory speculates."

Dr. Johannes raised his hand haltingly. "Some of you might be aware that I have long been a fan of pulp fiction and science fiction novels. Although most of you probably discount any of the ideas that have emerged from that controversial source, there has been some very interesting, speculative work concerning interstellar travel published there. In 1928, Kirk Meadowcroft published *The Invisible Bubble*, in which he proposed the idea of hyperspace, a realm or parallel universe in which it is possible to travel much faster than light."

"Three years later, in 1931, John Campbell published a short story entitled 'Islands of Space,' in which he championed the idea of intergalactic space vehicles traveling through the cosmos in a gravity well within which the craft doesn't violate the cosmic speed limit while the gravity well itself, which has no mass, does. The story was later updated and republished just a few years back in 1957."

"I've been tracking the recent work in this field. A theoretical physicist by the name of Alcubierre started work on a mathematical solution to the problem and developed what has come to be referred to as the Alcubierre warp drive. Although there are several serious obstacles to the practical application of his drive, the Alcubierre warp drive is a propulsion system that compresses time in front of a space craft and expands time to the rear after it has passed through. Thus, the craft is able to avoid the cosmic speed limit because it works entirely within a kind of temporal bubble. The space in front of the craft and following the craft is able to move much faster than the speed of light because it lacks mass, while the space ship operates at normal speed within the bubble well under the cosmic speed limit of the speed of light."

Dr. Atherton spoke up hesitatingly, "Is the Alcubierre Warp Drive a practical possibility right now today?"

"No sir, it is not. I think that it will take several more years, perhaps decades before the Alcubierre Drive will become a working reality."

Milton had been patiently listening to all of the team reports as they moved around the conference table. Finally, he spoke up and joined the conversation. "I was going to suggest that we take a hard look at the technology we've been trying to reverse engineer from the bridge control section of the alien craft in the lava tube cavern. That craft had to get here somehow from some astronomically distant place, and it suggests that they exceeded the speed limit of light limitations in doing so. I move that we adjourn until tomorrow so that I can prepare a presentation about an idea I have."

Milton woke up in a cold sweat the next morning, on the verge of stifling a scream in his throat, and startled Abigail awake.

"Are you feeling okay, Miltie?" Abigail asked sleepily.

"No, Abigail, I'm not. I had a terrible night's sleep. I kept dreaming about going down into the lava tubes to the cavern and wandering around the bridge of the alien ship. It was a nightmare!"

"Why would that be unsettling?"

"It's hard to explain. I kept moving around the bridge examining all of the technology and equipment that is still mounted in place that was too bulky or too heavy to take topside to the engineering labs. In my dream, I was looking for something, but I couldn't figure out what I was looking for."

"Do you know now?"

"No, it's still a big unknown. But I'm convinced that there must be something that we need to learn from the array of all the technology still on that bridge. There's something there that ties together many of the questions that we haven't yet resolved."

"Well," Abigail suggested, "I wouldn't let it ruin my day as well. It will come to you eventually, I'm sure. Perhaps it would help if you would tell me about your nightmare. What was it all about? How did it begin?"

"Maybe, you're right. Here, sit on the side of the bed with me, and I'll try to remember the detail from the dream."

"Do you remember where it all began?"

"Yes, I remember that quite well. It was frightening. I was wandering through the lava tubes trying to find my way to the cavern, and I kept getting turned around and lost in the maze of interconnecting tunnels. My claustrophobia overwhelmed me. Every time that I thought that I had figured it out and was on the right track to get there, I would find that I had somehow gotten turned around and I was back right where I had started. After what seemed like hours, I finally chanced upon the tube that led down to the cavern. I walked across the floor of the cavern and climbed up the ladder that the spelunker team had left in place, and entered into the bridge of the vessel. I remember that it required a strenuous effort, and I needed to sit down on an overturned crate and catch my breath."

"That by itself could be a little frightening."

"Yes, but then it began to get even more so. I got up from my perch and wandered around the outer ring of consoles that the ship's crew used to pilot the craft. Out of respect for the aliens, our teams had removed the bodies and given them a burial out on the floor of the cavern. They had even placed headstones identifying everyone as souls from the vessel wreckage. I paused at each console as I walked around the bridge, trying to sort out what was the purpose of all of the technology. I sat down in one of the over-sized chairs and pondered the organization of the bridge. I tried to imagine where the Commander of the craft would position his crew to run all of the technology in piloting the craft."

"You were able to figure that all out?"

"I think at least partially so. And then I passed out... or at least I think I did. I dreamed that I found myself in an active bridge where all of the alien crew were alive and hustling around the bridge performing their assigned responsibilities. I had a pretty good idea of where all of the technology that we had moved back through the lava tubes to the reverse engineering section in the base had been previously located, and I explored the bridge with my eyes trying to discern how the crew were using it. I think that I began to understand a little of what was going on, and then the Commander motioned excitedly to two crew members sitting side by side on the far side of the bridge to do something."

"Could you see what he was pointing at?"

"Intrigued, I got up and circled the bridge to where the crewmen were seated pushing buttons and pulling levers. I looked back across the Commander's chair and realized that the transparent screen portion of the craft that I had just entered through was now whole and complete. It provided a panoramic view of where the craft was going when underway. As the crewmen I was observing pushed buttons and moved levers, the viewscreen morphed a great deal and the former view on the cosmos changed... changed dramatically. It looked like we were speeding by astronomical bodies in the cosmos at an impossibly high speed."

"That must have been exciting to see."

"Yes, it was breathtaking.... Then suddenly, the craft appeared to have emerged from its precipitous flight in a large field of asteroids... a lot of asteroids in a wide swath... many more than we are familiar with today in our own asteroid belt. The two crewmen I was observing appeared to act in tandem like a combination of helmsman and navigator, moving the gigantic craft through the thick field of asteroids. But the craft was too large to maneuver, and the field of asteroids was too thick to move safely through, and, in spite of some apparent force field technology they were using, the asteroids began colliding with the ship's hull."

"The hull held, but one of the asteroids collided with the transparent viewing panel and cracked the screen. The Commander began gesticulating wildly and the navigator-helmsman team maneuvered the craft inside the asteroid ring in the direction of a blue green planet. As the crack in the viewing screen continued to widen, I could see that we were heading for an earthlike planet with a large pale moon circling it. Suddenly, the viewing panel gave way altogether and sucked out all of the interior atmosphere the aliens were breathing."

"The Commander issued one last command and slumped back in his chair as the craft approached the moon of the blue-green planet. The two navigator-helmsmen frantically pressed buttons and pulled levers and the whole craft momentarily dematerialized and then rematerialized inside the outer shell of the moon in the lava tube cavern."

"The whole nightmarish experience was so frightening that I think I passed out again. When I came to, the bridge was silent and the Commander and crew were all slumped over and appeared to be dead. I screamed in a panic, and that apparently was sufficient to wake me up from my nightmare. That was when you took me in your arms to comfort and console me. It took me quite a while to put the whole dream experience behind me."

"I think, Miltie, you don't want to put it behind you. You've been given an extraordinary gift of insight about how the alien craft was piloted and how it ended up in the cavern. I lost count of all the different technologies that were exercised in your nightmare. I'll bet that with your guidance, you can talk the reverse-engineering team through a whole bunch of solutions that have escaped us so far."

At the next propulsion team meeting, Milton led off the discussion. "In our last meeting, I heard a lot of ideas justifying why we don't have a workable propulsion system operational today. Perhaps in the role of ombudsman, let me take a few minutes to review the bidding on where we are at with a propulsion system for the ark.

One of the major problems we are facing is that the faster an object travels, the more massive it becomes. As an accelerating object gains mass and thus becomes heavier, it takes more and more energy to increase its speed. It would take an infinite amount of energy to make an object reach the speed of light. According to Einstein's theory of special relativity, exceeding the speed of light is impossible, as nothing with mass can travel faster than the speed of light in a vacuum. That's the universal cosmic speed limit... only massless particles like photons can travel at that speed."

Milton paused to catch his breath and then continued. "So, we are moving up a blind alley when we discuss propulsion strategies that all lead us up to the cosmic speed limit. Kepler 452b is 1402 light years away. It would take the ark at least fifteen hundred years to reach Kepler even if we were able to accelerate the ark's speed to just below the speed of light. Any such strategy is a non-starter before we even begin."

Dr. Atherton responded to Milton's dismal reminder about the cosmic speed limit. "I think we all understand that, Milton. But then what are we to do? It sounds like a catch-22, a cosmological impasse. We appear to be headed down a dead-end street."

"Be patient with me for a moment, everyone," Milton urged. "That's the point I'm getting around to addressing. We know that the alien craft had to break the cosmic speed limit to travel from wherever it came just to get here. That's a given. We just have to figure out how they did it. I would like to propose a possibility we haven't yet discussed. I had a night vision last night that suggests to me an option. I'm not too sure about all of the details but it seems to me that what we have to do is step outside the constraints of our physical reality and move to an alternate reality or dimension where we can momentarily maneuver the ark to the near vicinity of Kepler 452b, and then reemerge ready to go down and explore the planet for colonization. In other words, to get to Kepler 452b, we have to bypass all of the intervening space between Earth and our destination and leapfrog there."

"Excuse me, Milton," Dr. Patel interjected, "but that sounds like a fantasy... a fairy story. How can we move outside our own reality to another dimension?"

"That's a legitimate question, Dr. Patel." Milton responded. "That's what my night vision revealed. It all has to do with the evidence of the alien vessel in the cavern. It got there somehow. Its very existence in the cavern begs three important issues. First, the vessel obviously isn't of Earth manufacture, and it probably had to come across a great distance to get here. Second, with the exception of the broken observation screen at the front end of the bridge, the vessel is essentially intact. We've got to ask the question of how did it get inside the cavern. It just barely fits and yet there's no evidence of a break or scrape in the walls of the sides of the lava dome cavern."

Milton continued, "There are probably other possible factors at work here, but the one that invaded my night vision was that the aliens had a technology for leaving our temporal existence momentarily for another dimension, and then reappearing a moment later in a different place than where they just were. That kind of capability would also help explain the incredible maneuverability that UFOs have been demonstrating in standoffs with our Air Force on Earth... making 90-degree angle turns, traveling impossible speeds, and frequently simply disappearing from view when our fighter jets get too close when they are scrambled to investigate."

"That sounds so implausible," Dr. Patel argued. "We don't have any evidence of that kind of capability."

"Oh, but we do. That is precisely what I experienced in my night vision. I know this is a stretch for most of you, but the aliens were alive in my dream, and I watched them work the controls of their technology to make it happen."

"You watched them at work?... You saw it all?" exclaimed Dr. Atherton.

"That I did, sir. I don't understand it, but I did. I watched closely, and carefully noted all of the control panels... all of the buttons and levers...

that the aliens manipulated to do it. I am prepared to conduct a tour of the now defunct bridge and show you just which pieces of technology control interdimensional travel. If we have time, I think that I can also reconstruct which panels the aliens used for controlling the ship's force fields, deflector shields, and large frame antigravity fields. Are you all up for a little stroll down the lava tube to get to the cavern and the alien craft? We've got a lot of work to do to reverse-engineer alien technology, and we've got a steep learning curve to be able to understand how to use it."

"But what's the third issue? You said that there were three."

"That's right," Milton responded. "It's a blinding glimpse of the obvious. When the screen at the front end of the vessel was broken, the ship's commander and all of the crew members on the bridge apparently stayed at their stations and perished shortly after that. But let's not forget, the vessel has compartments and decks to accommodate thousands of passengers and other crew members. We haven't found any skeletons or mummified remains of any of them in the rest of the vessel. What happened to them? Where did they go?"

Chapter 14

While making his rounds one morning reviewing the progress of construction crews, Milton chanced upon an interesting communication conundrum. Several engineers and workers were on their break and were arguing about what language should be the official communication language on the lunar base and ark operations, and even beyond once the actual colonization work had begun on Kepler 452b. The discussion had erupted because so many of the engineers at work on the construction of the ark spoke English as a second language and many were more comfortable speaking in their native tongue.

It's true, it was argued, that English is the international language of aviation, but with the globalization of world commerce, many conversations conducted between pilots, ground crews, and air traffic controllers in purely domestic settings were conducted in the native language of that country. For instance, one Ph.D. engineer who was born in China but did his postgraduate work at Harvard, argued that flight controllers in China used English for international flights, but for most domestic flights in China, Mandarin Chinese was the language of choice.

A counter-argument was proposed by an engineer from Taiwan who pointed out that even for many flights between two non-English speaking countries, pilots would probably be using English. Moreover, even in mainland China, English is still the spoken language at many major airports.

The discussion took Milton by surprise. He had attended many global business conferences and educational post-graduate programs where multiple languages crept into the professional conversations. It seemed to him that although it sometimes slowed down the communication flow, it just as frequently increased the lucidity of communication because the multi-language approach created a much richer level of understanding.

When the engineers spied Milton, they attempted to drag him into the conversation. Milton wisely chose to avoid the argument for now, but made a mental note to bring together language specialty teams for a thorough examination of the subject. He was particularly concerned about getting communication issues out on the table now that would probably occur during flight of the ark and after the ark had landed on Kepler 452b.

The combined communication team meeting convened a few days later. In attendance were construction engineers, librarians, historians, archivists, IT specialists, and media types. They came at the topic from all different directions. The librarians, historians, and archivists were much concerned about preserving Earth's diversity of languages. They were hard at work assembling the wealth of human history into a workable package so that the colonists had easy access wherever they would settle on their new planet. They were adamant about avoiding the creation of dead languages, languages that no one any longer understood. They were most aware of all human progress being thwarted in the past by potentates and armies when they obliterated any trace of the ancient languages that knowledge and new learning had been captured in.

For that very reason, there were some factions at the meeting who were in favor of selecting Latin as the language of colonization. That way, everyone would have a vested interest in preserving ancient knowledge. The Chinese and other Asian participants were, of course, against that motion. They counter-proposed a dialect of Chinese as the language of choice for the colonists. That motion was immediately opposed by all the

Indo-European language groups present as it was the general position of most that Chinese was simply much too difficult to learn.

An intriguing proposal that took Milton by surprise was by a small contingent of former college professors who suggested that we ignore English, Chinese, and all of the other modern languages for our official language on the ark and Kepler 452b, and just switch over to Esperanto, a manufactured, artificial language.

Reference to Esperanto puzzled Milton. He immediately called Abigail on his walkie-talkie to see if she could join him at the meeting. She arrived a few minutes later. Milton quickly brought her up to speed on the meeting and asked for her views on Esperanto. Abigail had studied Esperanto during her graduate work at the university, and she motioned Milton to step away from the meeting to the side of the room where she could unobtrusively share ideas she had gleaned from the experience without interrupting the flow of the conversation in the meeting. Abigail had a functional eidetic memory and began to recite one of the essays she had written for a school assignment in her graduate program.

"Esperanto is a constructed auxiliary language. It was created in 1887. There was considerable excitement about it when it first appeared, but it never quite achieved the traction that its creators had intended. Esperanto derives predominantly from the Indo-European language groups. Approximately 80% is based on Romance languages but it also shares elements of Germanic, Greek, and Slavik languages. The two major advantages of Esperanto are its economical use of words, that is, you can say more with a reduced vocabulary, and it is claimed that it can be easily mastered in three to four months."

"Did you ever try to prove that out?" Milton queried.

"You mean trying to learn Esperanto in three or four months... Yes, as a matter of fact, I did. It took me about a month and a half to speak understandable conversational Esperanto and another two months to have mastered it sufficiently to write my semester paper in Esperanto. I got an A on the paper and was awarded by my professor a certificate identifying me as an advanced level Esperantist."

"I wonder, could you speak a few phrases in Esperanto for me so I can hear how it sounds."

"Sure. Here goes: Saluton. Kiel vi sanas? Kio estas via nomo? De kie vi estas? Agrablas renkonti vin."

"I'm impressed. I recognized some sound patterns but I think it would take me quite a bit longer than just three or four months to master it. I wonder how it escaped me that you were studying Esperanto so intently during our student years?"

"Because you always had your head in all your engineering books, silly."

Chapter 15

Milton and Abigail sat at the head of the conference table with Dr. Atherton and several historians, archeologists, and forensic scientists who were working together with other teams rolling together the narrative of American history.

"Tell us again your idea about the giant aliens from the vessel in the cavern, Milton," Dr. Atherton urged. "I get the idea that it is most important."

"Certainly, sir. The alien vessel was piloted by a group of very tall extraterrestrials. Many were as tall as ten feet or more. Most had six digits on their hands and feet, had a double row of teeth in their jaws, and sported a shock of red hair on their heads. Notwithstanding these differences from normal human beings, DNA analysis suggests that they were human in every regard."

"Yes, I think we've all read the reports on the crew at their posts in the bridge of the vessel."

"Yes, but what we've been ignoring all along is that the vessel was an ark designed to carry upwards of several thousand individuals." Milton reminded them. "Although the crew on the bridge died at their posts, we haven't found any evidence of what happened to all of the passenger colonists in the rest of the vessel. Where did they go? What happened to them? I would like to explore one possibility for just a moment. Dr. Connolly, you are an expert in the history of the indigenous peoples of North America who populated the central portion of the continent for several thousand years. Can you briefly share some of your expertise about the Mound Builders."

"Of course, Milton," Dr. Connolly responded. "We actually don't know a great deal of detail about the Mound Builders. Archeological studies have concluded that they built mounds over a period as long as 5,000 years. The term 'Mound Builders' doesn't necessarily refer to a specific culture or tribal group of people… it refers to their universal practice of building mounds… mostly burial mounds and effigy mounds. As the American pioneers started their push westward, they encountered thousands of mounds spread out all over the countryside from Ohio and on into the great Midwest. My personal favorite has long been the Serpent Mound in today's Peebles, Ohio. It's a great effigy mound. We don't know who built it or why. That's part of the mystique for the Serpent Mound and all of the other mounds we have encountered in the Ohio River Valley and along the Upper Mississippi River."

"As miners started digging for coal and other minerals and as settlers started knocking down the mounds to prepare fields for planting, they occasionally encountered the bones of very tall people, many with six digits on hands and feet, double rows of teeth and shocks of red hair, all mixed in together with a much greater number of normal-sized people. Today, established science discounts the evidence of giants encountered as reported in the early newspapers that sprang up in the 1800s and early 1900s."

"And what is your read on all this, Dr. Connolly?"

"Well, up until my field work experience here on the lunar base, I was convinced that, like my peers in the field of archaeology, the majority of the early pioneer reports were exaggerations of what the early settlers and miners found when they broke ground. That is, the stories of a remnant of a race of giants who had once populated the land were mostly bogus. Today, I'm not quite so sure. There appears to be a correlation between the people on the ark down in the cavern, and the stories of a remnant of a giant race of people who once inhabited the region of the Great Plains of North America and other locations on Planet Earth."

"I understand. Thank you. Now, we don't really need to get embroiled in an archeological dispute about the settlement patterns of North America. What I am leading up to is the possibility that the colonists on the ark in the cavern managed to leave the Ark and get down to Earth's surface and do so without so much as leaving any openings in the ark superstructure or outer hull plating. That begs the question of how did they do it. I believe the answer is much simpler than we might suppose."

"What do you mean, Milton?" Dr. Atherton asked.

"Well, we already know something about the technology that those ancients used to disassociate themselves from our reality once their ark was irretrievably damaged, and reassociate the ark within the confines of the cavern. Their technology was powerful enough to move the entire ark through an alternate reality dimension and then back again. I am proposing that they employed that same technology to move the entire population of colonists down dirtside to Planet Earth. I suspect that they didn't do it in mass but with miniaturized versions of the technology like we encountered on the alien bridge to move individuals or small groups at a time. I propose that we deploy a team of engineers and scientists experienced in reverse-engineering alien technology to explore the ark cabins to see what secrets we might have missed. I suspect we'll find what we're looking for repeated a thousand times over on the twenty-some decks of the vessel."

Chapter 16

Dr. Atherton quickly organized a joint team of archeologists, reverse engineers, and assorted scientists interested in the possibilities of multiple dimensions, and sent them on a mission back to the alien vessel, this time to search individual quarters for technology to traverse dimensions.

"They didn't have to look far," Dr. Atherton reported back to Milton. "Once they knew what they were looking for, they found that virtually every set of quarters had a miniaturized version of the apparatus that we found on the bridge. The team hypothesized that this was the alien colonists' escape measure to abandon the vessel in case of emergency."

"That's just what I anticipated." Milton responded. "Did they find the technology still operational? That would make it much easier to reverse engineer it for use on our own ark."

"Yes, unfortunately, they discovered that it was still operational quite by accident. A team of archaeologists, Steve Baird, Andre Bordeau, and Enrique Salazar, were examining the layout of one of the sets of quarters on deck three of the alien ark. None of them had participated in the initial examination of the dimensional transfer technology on the bridge and weren't familiar with how it was configured or how it worked."

"The team encountered a bank of digital technology mounted on one wall of the passenger cabin. Dr. Baird approached the unfamiliar apparatus, extending his hand to touch a small lever on the face of the mechanism. He immediately disappeared. Bordeau and Salazar were across the room examining something when it happened and when they realized what happened with Dr. Baird, they charged over to where he had been standing and attempted to find him. Dr. Bordeau arrived first and unintentionally touched the same lever on the apparatus that Dr. Baird had energized, and Bordeau disappeared. Salazar was only one step behind Dr. Bordeau, and when he touched the apparatus, he followed suit and disappeared as well."

"The fourth member of the search team for that cabin, Dr. Stanley Brisket, was standing in the hatchway entrance and observed all that had transpired. He alerted the rest of the search teams on the vessel and explained what he had witnessed. They immediately decided to dispense with the search for the technology until they knew more about how the dimensional transference technology worked."

"So, three members of one of our search teams, Baird, Bordeau, and Salazar, all were snatched up by dimensional transference technology and disappeared," Milton summarized. "Do we know what happened with them? Where did they go?"

"Yes, and that's the interesting part," responded Dr. Atherton. "Dr. Bordeau ended up in the Iraqi desert within walking distance of the shores of the Euphrates River. He was encountered by a team of American soldiers who were operating on patrol in the area and quickly transported him to their base headquarters where he was processed and loaded on a military transport back to the United States. Dr. Salazar rematerialized in West Germany near Mainz in the middle of a wine vineyard. The vineyard owner contacted American authorities at a nearby military base, and he too was soon on his way back to the United States."

"What about Dr. Baird?"

"Dr. Baird presents a special case."

"Special case? What do you mean? Don't keep me in suspense... Where did he turn up?"

"It was almost the worst possible of cases. He materialized inside the security fence line at Fort Knox, Kentucky."

"Fort Knox? You mean where much of the gold in the United States is stored and guarded?"

"That's right. The soldiers providing perimeter security for Fort Knox immediately detected him and one surprised soldier fired his weapon, wounding Dr. Baird in the chest. They evacuated him to the base hospital and performed emergency surgery trying to save his life."

"That's bad... that's very bad! How is he doing? Is he going to recover?"

"Thankfully yes. Recovery is going to take some time. However, it appears that he has no memory of the experience or how he got there inside the restricted cantonment area at Knox."

"Have the other two any memory of what happened to them?"

"Yes, and that's where it gets really interesting. They have quite vivid recollections of what transpired when the dimensional transference technology snatched them out of the alien vessel and deposited them at random places on earth. Both of them report that as soon as the technology grabbed them, they found themselves in a nondescript place where normal time didn't seem to happen. Neither was able to conjecture how long they were in this in-between place before they suddenly found themselves on earth in the Iraqi desert and the Mainz vineyard. From their perspective, it might have been mere seconds or it might have been days or weeks. There simply was no way to measure the passage of time."

Chapter 17

Milton, Abigail and Dr. Atherton were seated in the lunar base conference room with a thick sheaf of papers spread out across the conference table. "It seems to me," Abigail observed, "that we have covered most, if not all, of the most important areas that we need to nail down as we prepare for the maiden voyage of the ark."

"You mean the ONLY voyage of the ark, Abigail," Milton chuckled. "We only get one shot at it."

"Yes, you're right of course."

"But," Abigail observed, "it might be prudent for us to lay out here on the table every area we have observed and any observations we might have about what we saw that still need our attention."

"That sounds logical to me. What do you think Dr. Atherton?"

"Yes, I agree. I have a premonition that all the areas are not as well prepared at this point as we would hope for. Ark launch date is less than a year away now, and I think we may be behind in some significant areas."

"Let's look at the big picture first," Milton suggested. "A holistic view will keep us informed on how the individual sections are preparing and the effectiveness of how well all of the sections are interconnected, interrelated, and interdependent."

Dr. Atherton spoke up, "May I propose a set of metaphors to get the ball rolling. The organization for the ark is very similar to how nuclear submarines or cruise ships are put together. They're all very much enclosed, self-sufficient communities. Our ark is much like them in many ways. However, our ark is several orders of magnitude larger and more complex in its planning and execution. Let's go through each of the sections of the ark one by one."

Milton said, "Let me lead off with some of my observations. I did a walk-through of the bridge as the engineers finished with all of the technology installation. They were very thorough in testing out all of the systems and control panels. It looked to me like it's about ready to go."

Abigail followed up with comments about the flora and fauna that will be transported on the ark. "Although the plants and animals that we will take with us on the ark appear to be the simplest of ark requirements, it is probably one of the most complex and sophisticated of our tasks. It's not just a matter of gathering up and cataloging a broad inventory of plants and animals to jump start life on the new planet. We have to be extra careful with what we bring on board to ensure that we don't inadvertently allow entry to nasty critters and toxic plants that will thwart our settling options in our new environment aboard the ark or dirtside on Kepler 452b."

"Consequently, I suggested that we set up a special warehouse triage sorting point to inspect every plant and animal for vectors and toxicity before they were loaded on the ark. All of the teams responsible for plant and animal husbandry have been hard at work in meeting that requirement. They've also been running models to make sure that the combination of plants and animals selected to come with us are compatible. This testing, of course, applies to all potential colonists to ensure that they don't harbor any viruses or disease that could cause a major epidemic or pandemic in our new home. We've set up a special laboratory for testing all plants, animals, and humans on a regular basis to make sure that we haven't missed anything."

"Figuring out how to pollinate all the crops being grown at the lunar base, and eventually on the ark, had been both necessary and problematic.

Luckily, honeybees had already developed the needed skills, so the only problem to be solved was how to maintain beehives in space. The apiarists were in charge of this task. They had taken steps to maximize the genetic diversity in the queens in each of the 50 hives currently aboard the lunar base. The ark was also being outfitted with all the equipment necessary to maintain the hives and also keep a supply of genetically diverse queens available for the long flight to Kepler 452b."

"As an aside Milton," Dr. Atherton suggested, "we're going to have you and Abigail thoroughly checked out to ensure that you don't harbor any lingering polio virus in your systems. If you do, then you won't be able to depart when the ark launches."

Milton grimaced and paused, but continued his report on the status of languages among the colonists. "Effective communication in a multilingual environment like our colonists represent is of great importance. I attended several meetings of linguists, historians, librarians, ethnologists, archivists, and philologists. They are well aware that language is not a static thing. It is constantly evolving and morphing. They have set up a team to keep a constant vigil lookout for the evolution of language in the relatively enclosed speech environment of the ark and the new planet. They are organized to track phonology, sound patterns and changes; morphology, word structure, and syntax, linguistic meaning. But no matter how closely they track potential for language change, I suspect that they'll have their work cut out for them during the ark's journey and once we get to Kepler 452b and the colonists spread out over the land."

"For right now, the librarians and archivists are putting together a digital Hall of Records with technology that will be able to read and interpret records in whatever recording medium is developed and implemented. Included in that package will be a digitally formatted Rosetta Stone so that we will always be able to work across language groups with understanding."

"The linguists spent quite a while debating language and selecting the language that would become the standard for the ark's journey and for the colonist communities once we have landed when we get there. There was quite a bit of discussion and thrashing about as scientists from different language groups lobbied for their native tongue."

Abigail added, "Don't forget that there was also some discussion about Esperanto. Several of the delegates to the language team had studied Esperanto at one time or another and suggested that selecting it might be the best solution for eliminating arguments about a uniform language for all."

Milton observed, "Since long discussions on the topic didn't produce any useful insights or a decision on a universal language, it was decided to just let language evolution take whatever direction and course that naturally occurs."

Dr. Atherton spoke up. "Did the team give any consideration for International Sign language or American Sign Language. I believe we have a significant group of colonists who are deaf and would benefit from some agreed-upon standard."

"Good point, sir." Abigail said. "No, they did not. I'll take that one on at the next team meeting of the minds on language and see what they come up with."

Because of his graduate work in aeronautical engineering, Milton spent the majority of his time working with the engineering teams that designed the ark and the construction teams that assembled it. In spite of his claustrophobia, he spent much time wandering through the bridge of the alien vessel and on back through the many kilometers of passenger quarters, plant and animal areas, and electrical, water, air circulation, and sanitation systems. He was particularly observant of how the aliens had designed the living quarters for the individual passengers and families.

In this regard, the design of the ancient vessel was much like a modern multi-deck cruise ship. Many of the workers on the ark construction crew had previously worked Earthside on the construction of the giant cruise ships. This greatly facilitated moving the work forward toward completion.

In a little less than ten years, they had completed work on the bridge and twenty-five decks of colonist cabins. In another five years, they completed work on all of the utility elements of the ark and it was quickly nearing overall completion.

Chapter 18

The day finally arrived for the colonist passenger final boarding. The colonists responsible for all the animals and plants had finished loading after several months of vetting. Milton and Abigail underwent strenuous testing to ensure that they weren't carriers of the polio virus. They were given a clean bill of health and so they proceeded to make their cabin livable for the duration of the voyage. All of the colonists had spent the previous weeks loading their personal effects they wanted to take with them.

Because the dimensional transference technology had reduced the anticipated ark journey time from 1400 years to a mere year at the most, work on the cryogenic technology was abandoned and it was determined that all ark personnel and colonists would remain conscious throughout the journey.

Captain Bart Abernathy, a former U.S. submarine commander, was selected to lead the ark expedition as its captain at the helm. Abernathy and his bridge crew had been undergoing simulation training for the previous six months and were confident in their ability to maneuver the great ark through the cosmos.

As the launch date approached, the colonists and crew began to conduct individual departure parties celebrating the milestone of final mission readiness. When all was ready, all of the colonists and crew retired to their quarters and prepared for launch. The reverse-engineering team had been hard at work developing a miniaturized version of the dimensional transference technology, but it was determined that the system might be unreliable in an emergency. Instead, although all cabins and posts in the ark were outfitted with the miniaturized temporal transference apparatus equipment, they also relied on auxiliary emergency evacuation systems that depended on individual escape pod in each cabin and a system of oversized parachutes to lower the pods and evacuees safely to the ground once they had been jettisoned from the ark.

When it came time to launch, Captain Abernathy held a ceremony in the main ark conference room at which Mr. Drexel made a few brief congratulatory remarks and wished everyone a safe journey. At the conclusion of his formal remarks, he embraced Abigail and Milton with prolonged hugs and kisses. Then, with great fanfare and applause by all present, Mr. Drexel performed his last official duty before the ark launched… he remotely released a Goliath-sized bottle of champagne from a small launch platform positioned adjacent to the ark which floated in zero gravity and smashed into the bow of the ark. As the champagne bottle shattered and splashed its contents out into the ether, a resounding cheer went up from all the workers and colonists. The ceremony was transmitted by video hook-up to all of the compartments on the ark, and every team had a supplemental departure gathering with toasts and goodbyes. Then, everyone had just thirty minutes to get to their departure locations, and as the bridge sounded a departure warning alarm bell, the huge ark pulled away from the drydock moorings and moved slowly out into open space.

The ark design didn't rely on wormholes, nuclear power, or liquid fuels for its primary propulsion during the journey to Kepler 452b Instead it was designed to move the ark primarily across the cosmos using the ark's central dimensional transference apparatus. With the combined effects of the initial thrust and final slowdown provided by traditional propulsion means, the journey was projected to take just a matter of a few days instead of the 1400-plus years if the ark were to have been held to the cosmic speed limit. Following departure from the lunar base construction site, the ark traveled briefly under traditional liquid hydrogen/oxygen power for one day to give the engineers an opportunity to check out all of the ark's propulsion systems.

When the engineers had a high degree of assurance that the ark's standard propulsion systems were all a 'go', they initiated the ark's-central-dimensional transference apparatus to close the gap with the distance to Kepler 452b traveling in hyperspace. The view from the bridge observation deck and the colonist's side windows in their cabins immediately went dark momentarily. Then, after just a short pause, the ark reemerged from hyperspace with the sphere of 452b filling everyone's observation windows.

Everything was going according to plan at that point in time, and the colonists were resting comfortably in their cabins waiting for the all-clear sign to begin an orderly descent down to the planet's surface. However, the planners hadn't taken into account the possibility that 452b might have a system of rings surrounding it, much like the rings of Saturn. The ark ran full conventional speed into the rings, and the deflector shields did little to protect the ark from imminent destruction.

The great ark began to disintegrate around them, as it plowed through the planet's complex ring system of billions of ice and rock particles. Milton and Abigail rushed to mount up in their assigned cabin escape pods. When they had strapped themselves in, each pushed the ejection button and their pods were thrown free of the craft through the now-open side panel just as the ark cleared the ring of debris surrounding Kepler 452b. They were now within the gravity well for the giant exoplanet, and their pods plummeted downward towards the planet's surface. All of the pods had been outfitted with small retro rockets to slow the initial descent down to the planet's surface. After a few brief moments of terror, the speed of the fall of their escape pods was further slowed by the automatic deployment of a set of three enormous parachutes.

Abigail's parachutes deployed first and jerked her escape pod back into the sky as Milton's pod continued its rapid descent past her towards the planet's surface. Milton was in a panic as he had to consider that his parachutes might not deploy in time to stop his descent before he crashed into the planet's rocky surface. He could see the ground rushing toward him through the pod's observation portal windows. Looking off in the distance, he observed thousands of individual escape pods break off in mass from the ark's main body and several enormous sections of the ark that had separated from the huge craft. These were the primary carriers for the ark's complement of botanical and zoological specimens to repopulate the planet.

One was a gigantic tanker for all the aquatic species they had brought with them. Each of these giant sections had its own set of anti-gravity generators and thrusters, and their descent was slow and gradual, notwithstanding their enormous size. Once they touched down, the zoological and botanical sections opened spontaneously as the exploding bolts holding the doors in place released all of their cargo onto the surface. Many of the now liberated animals stampeded out through the now-open cargo doors and rushed out across the land in all directions.

The aquatic section had a steering mechanism operated remotely by a team of marine biologists. Their job was to steer the descent of the tanker and bring it down in a water environment where the aquatic creatures could break free and swim away from the now derelict craft.

In spite of his precarious position plummeting toward the planet's surface, Milton felt a sense of satisfaction to see that the escape mechanisms he had engineered into the ark's emergency escape modules had functioned so well. Finally, he felt the jerking movement of his chutes above him as they billowed open, and the pod began to drift off to the side from the rocky land mass where he had assumed he would touch down.

With the change of direction, it appeared he was going into the water on the shoreline of an immense sea. Although Milton was well practiced swimming in the indoor pool at the Drexel mansion and the exercise pool on the lunar base, he knew that he didn't have the stamina to swim any great distance to get to shore if it dropped him too far out to sea. In the final moments of its descent, the pod hovered above a formidable rocky outcropping that Milton was certain would rip the escape pod to shreds if it landed there.

But with only a few hundred feet or so to go, a gust of wind caught up in the chutes, altering the direction of descent and carrying the pod out over the water. The pod submerged momentarily into the surf and then bobbed up again to the surface as it deployed a ring of flotation balloons. Through the portal window, Milton could see the sandy beach not too far off from where the pod had touched down. Greatly relieved at his good fortune, Milton scrambled to unfasten himself from the chamber's automated restraint harness and wiring system and crawled out of the confining space of the chamber. As the restraining lock to the chamber access door clicked open, he pushed upward on the lid and slowly pulled himself up and out.

Dropping down over the side of the tank, he slogged through the shallow water of a tidal pool and made his way to the dry, sandy beach. He collapsed on the sand and lay there for a few minutes breathing hard and trying to get his bearings on the new planetary surface. Kepler 452b was slightly larger than Planet Earth and so he felt the much heavier pull of gravity on his body. The thicker atmosphere made breathing a little more difficult. He took a deep breath and confirmed that the atmosphere had about the right mix of oxygen, nitrogen, and hydrogen to make it completely breathable. Rolling over on his back, he looked up into the deep azure sky with wispy white clouds arrayed along the horizon.

Chapter 19

As he lay there on the sand, exhausted from the effort of breaking free from his metallic cocoon, another escape pod appeared in the sky directly above him, dropping toward the ground in a broad arc, suspended also by three enormous parachutes. The new chamber landed just a few dozen meters away in the same pool Milton had just climbed out of. When the lid of the newly arrived chamber opened, Milton spied Abigail, the true love of his life.

Milton ran toward her through the shallow surf to wrap her up in his arms and embrace her, but he tripped over a small rock hidden in the shallow water and took a header in the sand as the surf retreated. He lost his balance and fell, hitting his head on a rounded piece of volcanic rock, causing him to lose consciousness. As he gradually came around, he heard voices... familiar voices... from a time long past...

"I think he's finally going to come out of his coma and wake up. He's been out such a long time. His eye movement indicates that he must still be dreaming. He's been dreaming for twenty years now. That must be some dream! Someone, find Abigail quick. She will want to be here in case he actually does wake up"

Milton slowly opened his eyes and looked around. Two young orderlies stood there at the hatchway observation port on the side of his iron lung, apparently dumbfounded that he had just regained consciousness. Two mature gentlemen dressed in white lab coats with stethoscopes draped around their necks stood next to them expectantly. He scanned the embroidered names on their lab coats. With great surprise, he realized it was Jack and Sam, at least it was highly aged versions of them.

"Jack... Sam... where have you been?"

"Actually, Miltie," Jack spoke up. "We were just going to ask you the same question. It's been some twenty years now. Both of us are now practicing physicians specializing in polio and other attendant viral maladies. We've been working in the experimental laboratory in the clinic for many years. We've been waiting a long time for you to wake up."

Sam spoke up completing the thought, "We've witnessed you in a coma for two long decades now, lad. When you started to move this morning, we were hoping that this was finally the moment that you were going to break free and awaken. The wiring harness connected to your head resting on the pillow outside the iron lung had begun to pick up a great deal of electric activity and static and it looked very promising."

Milton's body stirred inside the metal canister and he began to move his head slowly from side to side. He was totally confused. He had been literally grabbed from the arms of his beloved on the shores of a giant alien exoplanet and delivered back into the unwelcome embrace of an iron lung in what appeared to be his old polio recovery bay.

"Whhh... what... happened? How did I get back here? Am I dreaming? Where did Abigail go?"

"She just stepped out, Miltie. She said she would be right back." As he spoke, an attractive matronly woman with honey blonde hair now dimmed with years, wheeled through the doorway to the bay. She sensed everyone's excitement and hurried over to the side of Milton's iron lung. When she realized that he was conscious, she let out a triumphant whoop of relief. "Miltie... Miltie... You're back... after so many years away, you're finally back." Tears flooded her eyes and rolled down her cheeks.

Milton was totally confused. "Excuse me, Ma'am, but just who are you? Are you Abigail's grandmother?"

The woman laughed and the tears came uncontrollably now. "No silly, it's me... it's Abigail... I'm me... you've been out of it in a deep coma for a very long time... twenty years... oh, a very long twenty years. I've missed you so much, Miltie!"

"But how is that possible? I'm still me. I haven't changed."

"Oh, but you have Miltie... you have. Quite a bit."

As if on cue, the orderly standing to the side of the woman stepped forward and set a basin of soapy water down in front of her. She quickly washed her hands and dried them on the proffered towel as the orderly opened the side hatch door. She reached through and grabbed Milton's hands in her own. "It's me, Miltie, it's really me. It's Abigail... and this is you."

The orderly standing at the front end of the iron lung positioned a mirror so that Milton could see himself. What he saw was a mature man, beginning to gray at the temples, who reminded Milton a great deal of his father.

"That's me? But what happened? I was young just a few minutes ago!"

"Oh, Miltie, you've been asleep for over twenty years, and you have been dreaming the entire time. It was all a dream. I hope that it was mostly pleasant, but I am so happy to have you back again."

"But you were just with me on the shores of a distant exoplanet, light years away. We've never been apart."

"Oh, in a way we have always been together, but not like you think. After you fell and hit your head on the floor when you were practicing using the new cuirass equipment to free you up from the iron lung, you lost consciousness and you've been in a coma ever since,... for over twenty years now."

Milton scanned the polio bay with his eyes and realized that it was pretty much empty with the exception of his own iron lung. Puzzled, he looked over at Abigail.

"You're wondering where everyone has gone? Little by little, through the years, the polio patients here in the bay who were still trapped in their iron coffins died off or were healed sufficiently to go home or to some other facility. Until, finally, you were the only patient left here in the bay. Father donated a large contribution to the Polio Recovery Center, and they modified a special bedroom for me off to the side of the bay. My father convinced them to keep the bay fully operational in case there was another polio outbreak and it was needed."

"Was it?" Milton inquired with a mild sensation of dread.

"Fortunately, that never occurred… at least not yet." Abigail responded. "Unfortunately, there were quite a few of the early polio virus sufferers who apparently had healed through the administration of experimental drugs and lots of physical exercise early on, but suffered through post-polio syndrome later in life as they aged."

"Post-polio syndrome? What's that?"

"Well, Miltie, it's the latent symptoms of poliomyelitis that don't appear until later in life, caused by the damaging effects of the viral infection on the nervous system in the patients' youth."

"Symptoms… what kind of symptoms?"

"Well, there are quite a few… muscle and joint weakness and pain that gets worse as we age, atrophying muscle tissue, fatigue and exhaustion, sometimes breathing and swallowing problems, and even sleep disorders called sleep apnea."

Milton considered all this new information and sighed, "I'm so glad that you managed to avoid all that, Abigail."

"Actually, Miltie, I didn't." Abigail wheeled her wheel chair around to the front of Milton's iron lung where he could see that she was now confined once again to a wheel chair. I was fine for many years, but it gradually caught up with me."

"I'm so sorry, Abigail. Is it painful?"

"Not really, Miltie… just terribly exhausting and sometimes it hurts to breathe."

Milton tried to change the subject. "You are fortunate that you have had your father to look out for you and provide for your needs."

"Oh, Daddy worked closely with the polio center, setting up a small bedroom for me just off the central bay where I could be close to you full time."

"But what do you do here to keep from going crazy with inactivity?"

"I've never been inactive, Miltie. I've been sitting here by the side of your iron lung reading to you from all the great and not-so-great classics. Twenty years of reading has allowed me to share with you a great deal of literature. It has been a labor of love."

Just then, two additional men entered the bay and approached Milton's canister. Milton turned his head toward them. Startled, he realized it was Captain Bill Rothwell and his crew member who ran the shuttle rocket back and forth from the moon construction site. Rothwell's hair was beginning to turn gray at the temples.

"We were just about to leave the building when they caught up with us and asked us to come down to the polio bay."

"Captain ... Rothwell... Bill... what are you doing here?"

"Excuse me, sir. I don't believe we've ever met."

"Oh, but we have. I spent a lot of time on your rocket express shuttling back and forth from the moon."

"You know about the shuttle and the moon base?"

"Know about it? I lived there for a good many years working primarily with the engineers to develop the ark systems necessary to travel across the immensity of space to Keplar 452b."

Captain Rothwell looked slightly bewildered. Turning to the head resident who had just walked in, "I think you better find Dr. Atherton and get him here quickly. I just ferried him in on the last shuttle and drove him over here to the polio center to drop him off. I think he was headed in the direction of your office. We need to find out what's going on here."

Milton was outfitted with his old cuirass and found that it fit him rather well after all the time that had passed. He wore the cuirass as he sat at a conference table that had been set up at the far end of the polio bay. Surrounding the table were Abigail, Mr. Drexel, Dr. Atherton, Captain Rothwell, and several of the scientists and project engineers who happened to be earthside at the moment.

Mr. Drexel chaired the meeting. "Good morning, Miltie. It's good seeing you again. You have brought that old sparkle back to my daughter's eyes. It's such a great blessing for her... and for us all. We have some questions for you this morning if you feel up to it. If it tires you too much, we can adjourn and reconvene at a later time. Dr. Atherton, I believe we should start with you and work our way around the table..."

Dr. Atherton paused for a few minutes as if trying to figure out how to proceed. "Let me get this straight, Milton. As I understand it, you can remember everything that you experienced in your dreams while you were in a coma these past twenty years. And your dreams resulted in an accurate understanding of everything that has transpired on the lunar base in the construction of the ark during those past twenty years?"

"Well, I don't know about everything, but I remember a lot."

"Let me come at my questioning from a different direction. You say that you participated in the operation of the lunar base and construction of the ark during the entire time you were asleep in a coma. Is that right?"

"Yes, sir... that about sums it up."

"Twenty years-worth of memories... What projects did you work on?"

"Well, let's see... lack of gravity, muscle degeneration and atrophy, long-range therapies for muscle and bone atrophy, resistance exercise and muscle toning, electric muscle stimulation, various approaches to artificial gravity, alternate realities, dimensional transference and the multiverse, antigravity, force fields, deflector shields, induced cryogenic sleep and sleep chambers, and on the hard science side of things, propulsion systems, ark component systems, metallurgy and ark construction. That's a good start for now. I think that you can jar my memory by just asking me questions."

Another engineer that Milton remembered well from his coma dreams spoke up. "Are you telling us that you worked on the ark propulsion and strategies for overcoming the immense distances of space?"

"Actually Bob, we worked together for several years on just those issues."

Another scientist at the table interrupted, "How about food and water recycling systems... hydroponic, bioponic, and aquaponic systems?"

"Yes, sir, all of those."

Dr. Atherton turned to the young man sitting next to him at the table who was frantically writing, trying to capture everything that was said. "Did you capture most of that conversation, Jimmy? I have a feeling that we're in way over our heads, and mine is spinning, but we've got to have a starting point."

Turning back to Milton, Dr. Atherton raised an important point. "What concerns me most Milton is just what do we get from your twenty-years-worth of dreaming. Does any of it track with reality... is any of it meaningful for our work today?"

"You'll have to answer that question Dr. Atherton. I would have no way of knowing."

"You're of course right, Milton. That was clumsy of me. Let's devise a little test for a metric to see what advantage your dreams give us."

"I think I have just the ticket, Dr. Atherton, but it may take a couple of days to prove out. The lunar base was built in the near vicinity of an ancient volcano, now dormant. The volcano created a complex system of lava tubes that go on for miles. At the end of one of the tubes, a team of base spelunkers discovered an ancient intergalactic vessel in an enormous cavern. At the time, they estimated that it had been there for over 15 to 20 thousand years. The control section in the bridge of the vessel was loaded with all kinds of technology unfamiliar to us. One of them was antigravity. Josh... Captain Parker, as moon base commander, if you would please dispatch a team of spelunkers and engineers armed with ultra bright flashlights into the tubes, I think you'll find that what I am saying is true."

"You're saying that we weren't the first on the moon... that an alien vessel is buried deep in the lava tubes near our lunar base site?"

"That's about it, sir. Travel time on foot through the tubes from the lunar base to the alien vessel takes about 30 minutes. Your team may have a difficult time finding their way through the tubes, but it shouldn't take them too much time beyond that. Please tell them to mark the track of their path through the tubes so they don't get lost along the way. Have them radio back when they have located the cavern with the alien vessel, and I will talk them through what we found in my dream."

Dr. Atherton sat there quietly considering what Milton had just revealed about an ancient alien spacecraft buried deep in the lava tubes on the far side of the moon. Finally, he reluctantly acknowledged, "I guess that blows the Fermi Paradox out of the water."

"Fermi Paradox?" Captain Rothwell queried. "What's that?"

Dr. Atherton chuckled and quickly responded, "Given the vastness of space and all of the trillions of celestial bodies that we have discovered viewing the cosmos with the new powerful telescopes we have at our disposition today, the paradox is that we haven't yet come across any intelligent life elsewhere. We seem to be alone in the universe."

Abigail sat quietly at Milton's side through all the give-and-take of the questioning. But then, her ears perked up when Milton brought up one additional item that hadn't been mentioned thus far.

"Abigail and I were married early on in the project, and we lived as husband and wife for most of the twenty years."

That revelation took Atherton's breath away. "You're married? Who performed the marriage?"

"Why Captain Parker, the Lunar Base Commander."

All eyes in the room turned to stare at the Commander.

Milton continued, "It was a simple ceremony. Mr. Drexel gave the bride away by video hookup, and several of you sitting around the table were also present. We had a blowout reception celebration in one of the base's large bays to follow it up."

Milton paused. There was dead silence in the conference room. Everyone's eyes turned back to Captain Parker. He in turn returned the gaze to Dr. Atherton. Dr. Atherton and Mr. Drexel were just beaming and leaning forward in their seats. Captain Parker was befuddled. "Just what do you want me to do about that, Dr. Atherton… Mr. Drexel?"

"Why, I want you to immediately confirm the marriage vows already taken by this couple. I know that the circumstances are a bit unusual but unusual times call for unusual solutions. This seems to me to be just such a case."

"You know that I legally can only perform marriages when we are underway in space or set up at the lunar base. That would probably violate the letter of the law."

"Commander, please hang with me on this. I'm not asking you to *perform* a marriage. I'm just asking you to *confirm* the marriage already performed when Milton and Abigail were present on your lunar base in his dream coma."

"Well, that runs perilously close to the edge of the law, but I think that, considering Milton's near eidetic recall of the past twenty years, it probably warrants it."

The Commander stood and moved to the end of the conference table and announced, "Would the bride and groom please approach me in your chairs. Mr. Drexel, would you please take your place by your daughter's side to give the bride away. Everyone else in the room will serve as witnesses to the confirmation of this marriage."

And with that, the marriage confirmation ceremony proceeded, this time without a follow-on blowout reception. When the ceremony was completed, Captain Parker looked at his watch and asked, any word back from the lunar base about the alien vessel yet?"

At that moment, an aide to the Lunar Base Commander rushed into the room and broke into the conversation excitedly. "They just found it, sir. They say it's huge. Their searchlight flashlights are extremely powerful, but they don't begin to illuminate the extent of the size of the vessel. I can't wait to see it in person."

Dr. Atherton glanced at his watch. He was breaking out in a cold sweat. I've got some work to do putting together teams to check out all of the information Milton has shared with us thus far. However, it's getting a little late on a Friday afternoon. I recommend that we adjourn these proceedings and continue them early next Monday morning. That will give us additional time to assemble all of the engineers and scientists who can benefit from the knowledge that Milton has accrued during his sleep time in the coma. Captain Rothwell, please arrange to depart immediately for the lunar base to shuttle back here as many of the section heads and key personnel as you can safely carry. If necessary, make several trips."

Milton chimed in, "Oh, and please bring back two black and white striped T-shirts for Abigail and me. We ought to be in uniform."

Some folks in the room were puzzled by that request, but Captain Parker knew precisely what Milton was referring to. He smiled a broad toothy grin. That was proof enough for him that Milton knew what he was talking about from his coma-dream experience.

"As for our bride and groom, Mr. Drexel would you please escort Abigail and Milton to their honeymoon suite."

Milton looked puzzled for just a minute and then it dawned on him what the Dr. Atherton was saying. His face broke out in a smile from ear to ear as Mr. Drexel accompanied the happy couple to Abigail's private bedroom in the corner of the polio bay. As Abigail and Milton entered their makeshift matrimonial suite, Mr. Drexel quipped, "It's true. All good things do come to those who wait... sometimes, it just takes longer."

Chapter 20

After Milton and Abigail had departed, Dr. Atherton and the remainder of the scientist-engineer crowd stayed seated, all looking rather perplexed. Finally, Dr. Zahn spoke up with the "elephant-in-the-room" question that was on everyone's mind: "Dr. Atherton, what do you make of all this... this coincidence of events in Milton's dreams and the reality we live in here today? Is it just that, a happy coincidence or is there more to it than that?"

"Thank you, Dr. Zahn, for getting the big questions out on the table where we can consider them and all their implications. I for one am totally bewildered. I don't know what psychological or cosmic dynamics are at work here. I believe, however, that it isn't precisely a recent thing with Milton."

"What do you mean, Dr. Atherton?" Dr. Zahn asked.

"If my memory serves me well, Dr. Frederick told me a story about an incident that transpired when Milton first arrived here at the Polio Clinic. He somehow managed to create a physical cockroach and cockroach carapace out of his nightmares. But it wasn't a legitimate cockroach species that populates the earth today. It was a unique cockroach that didn't quite match up with all the physical characteristics of a true cockroach. It didn't match up with the thousands of possible physical forms that cockroaches can take today. In all respects, it was an alien lifeform that simply seemed to emerge from Milton's mind."

Dr. Magnus shuddered and shared a discomfiting thought, "I can imagine that that would be quite disturbing with the involuntary production of physical manifestations of our nightmares."

Dr. Atherton chortled and explained, "Well, that's the only report I am aware of concerning that kind of occurrence with Milton. I agree that if it were a frequent happening, it could become extremely uncomfortable for Milton and for those around him. For now, it appears to be a singular happening. But Milton's experience with the cockroach does serve to demonstrate a certain degree of what we might call paranormal powers that most of us typically don't experience. That's what makes this situation so difficult to understand."

Dr. Atherton continued, searching for the right words and developing a workable hypothesis on the run as he spoke, "It appears that while he was asleep in his twenty-year coma, he was experiencing life in a parallel universe. A parallel universe is a hypothetical universe that coexists with our own but is distinct in some way. The idea of parallel universes leads to multiverse theory and suggests that many such universes might exist in parallel to each other. It appears that Milton was living in a parallel universe… not just a standard parallel universe but one that is quantum entangled with our own."

"Is quantum entanglement a scientifically sound hypothesis?"

"No, Dr. Ulrich, there is no statistically significant evidence which has been found for the existence of parallel universes or quantum entanglement between people. Consequently, I believe that Milton presents a singular occurrence demonstrating that at least one parallel universe exists in tandem with our own."

"While Milton was asleep in a coma, he experienced pretty much a similar life pattern that we were experiencing in normal space-time. But, let me point out, although Milton's dreams during his coma appear to replicate our reality, they miss the mark on a number of important points. First, his dreams are chronologically out of sync. It appears that he experienced things there on the lunar base that we haven't yet experienced in our reality here. Second, it appears that he experienced a great number of things that we might not ever have experienced had we not followed up on Milton's lead during our questioning. His description of the alien vessel in the lava tube cavern is a case in point. His responses have the capacity to set us moving extremely fast on resolving problems and issues that have confronted us here in our reality. Why?... because in his dream reality, they have already confronted those problems and issues and resolved them."

Dr. Atherton scratched his head and concluded, "I am initially inclined to accept Milton's dreams as evidence of an alternate reality in the multiverse, one perhaps influenced by quantum entanglement."

Dr. Akers interrupted, "Excuse me Dr. Atherton, but I'm still not familiar with the concepts you just mentioned. What is a multiverse and what is quantum entanglement? Those ideas are outside my field."

Dr. Atherton paused and looked around the table. "Good point. Perhaps there are several folks here who haven't gotten into the concept of multiverse in their work yet. Let me see if I can simplify the idea for all. We live in a four-dimensional universe defined by three spatial dimensions and one time dimension. Einstein once postulated, perhaps in a humorous way, that time, as a fourth dimension, is what keeps everything from happening all at once. But there has been some serious research conducted about the possibility of there also being a fourth spatial dimension, where two similar things could be happening simultaneously, precisely in the same three-dimensional space."

"Are you talking about string theory, Dr. Atherton?"

"Yes, in part. String theory postulates that there might be as many as ten or eleven dimensions linked together in some significant way. I heard this metaphor describing string theory at a recent conference. The speaker asked the audience to consider a cable. From a distance, it appears to be a single, thick strand. Get right up next to it and you'll see that the cable is actually woven from thousands of metallic threads. The speaker concluded his presentation with this assertion, 'There's always greater complexity than meets the eye, and this hidden complexity might well conceal all those additional dimensions that we can't perceive with the human eye.'"

"What about quantum entanglement? How does that figure in the idea of a multiverse?"

"Physicists postulate that quantum entanglement occurs when two subatomic particles become linked or connected in such a way that their properties are dependent upon each other, no matter how far apart they are. This phenomenon has been observed in empirical studies and experiments. But it is a phenomenon that occurs at the subatomic level. Based on those findings, however, some researchers have raised the possibility that two human beings could become quantum entangled. There has been no empirical evidence for this, but Milton's dream world seems to provide ample evidence that such a possibility exists."

The spelunker and engineer team confirmed the discovery of the enormous alien vessel in the lava tube cavern, and many of the other details of the lunar base and ark construction. Milton spent the next full month... all day—every day... being debriefed by the team of scientists and engineers that Dr. Atherton and the Lunar Base Commander had assembled. Everything that Milton said during the questioning was recorded and videotaped. With every new concept and idea that Milton related, a member of the team would relay a question to the corresponding teams on the Lunar Base asking them to corroborate what Milton had just shared. So far, after almost four weeks of interviews, Milton was still batting a thousand. He never missed. He never overexaggerated a point and he always nailed the concept precisely.

At the end of a particularly long session of grueling questioning, Milton was pretty well tuckered out. As he finished fielding the last question, he adjusted the fit of his cuirass and slowly stood. He turned to address Dr. Atherton, who was chairing the sessions that day.

"You'll have to excuse me, sir. I'm just a little tired and I need to go lie down. I know that Abigail is tuckered out too. Perhaps we can continue the questioning tomorrow morning."

"Agreed, Miltie, but first, Mr. Drexel has requested to have a private conversation with you and his daughter."

Turning to the crowd around the table who were slowly moving towards the door, he requested, "Could we please clear the room expeditiously."

As soon as everyone had filed out leaving only Milton, Abigail, and her father, Mr. Drexel turned to Milton. "Miltie, you probably won't remember this, but shortly after your mother died, they brought you a stack of papers to sign. One of those papers assigned me as your guardian and financial advisor with the sale of the family's farm property. And then you took the tumble and have been away for twenty years. In those years, I have served as your investment counselor, and I want to apprise you now that your funds have accrued considerable interest and represent a healthy principal today. The bottom line is that you are a wealthy man... a very wealthy man."

Milton considered what Mr. Drexel had just explained and then asked, "Sir, would you be willing to continue in that role for now? I have no use or need for money that I'm aware of. Perhaps you could set up a charity or a foundation providing funds for hospitals and schools. Let's call it the 'Abigail Fund.' That ought to be sufficient."

"I would be pleased to continue in that role, Miltie. Would you please just annotate and sign the bottom of the original contract paperwork to set the wheels in motion with the lawyers and the banks."

Milton dutifully signed the paper, thanked Mr. Drexel for his oversight, and left the room hand in hand with Abigail in her wheel chair. Entering the makeshift bedroom, Milton gently helped Abigail out of her chair to sit down on the edge of their bed. Milton put his arm around Abigail, and they sat there together side-by-side in silence for several minutes. Then without exchanging any words, Milton kissed Abigail on the cheek and then on the other cheek for good measure, and helped her lean back onto her side of the bed, fluffing up her pillow. When he had her settled in comfortably, he walked around to the other side of the bed and lowered himself down by the side of his sweetheart. Still holding hands, they just lay there together on their backs in their embrace, staring up at the ceiling.

The next morning, the hospital steward who routinely provided meals for the couple to eat each day, reported at the door to their bedroom with a breakfast feast laid out on a covered roller tray. After knocking several times with no response, he cautiously opened the door a slit and looked in. Milton and Abigail were still there in bed lying on their backs. Only they were no longer staring at the ceiling. Their eyes were closed and they had a wisp of a smile on their faces.

Realizing that the couple wasn't entirely with it, he pushed the emergency red alert call button, and the polio hospital orderlies descended on the run to see what was the matter. When they opened the door all the way and entered the room, they found Milton and Abigail still sleeping. The chief orderly advanced to the other side of the bed and gently shook Milton's shoulder to awaken him, but to no avail. Neither Milton nor Abigail would wake up. They had descended once again into the dream world of a prolonged coma and wouldn't stir ever again.

For Milton and Abigail, life was wonderful. They awoke to lying on the beach sand on the alien exoplanet with a gigantic red sun beginning to reach up out of the sea on the distant horizon. Enthralled by such a glorious sunrise, Abigail quoted from Homer's *Odyssey* that she had been reading to Milton most recently, "'The rosy fingers of dawn'... It's just beautiful, Miltie! I think this is what Homer must have had in mind."

They jumped up and playfully chased each other around the shoreline, unencumbered by Abigail's wheelchair and Milton's cuirass. They ran through the edge of the shallow surf, splashing on each other as they went about washing off the sand that had adhered to their bodies lying there on the shore while they slept through the night.

Then they began strolling hand-in-hand, walking away from the shore, climbing slowly up the long gentle slope to a high plateau that overlooked the beachline.

At the summit, they were met by several of the colonist families from the Ark who were waiting for them there. Milton looked over at Abigail with loving eyes and beamed. He wrapped her up in his arms and gave her a long, warm embrace.

"Abigail, we're home at last."

Reflection

Although I contracted the polio virus as a child, this novel is not autobiographical. Ignoring the advice of the medical authorities of the day, my mother refused to have me interned in an iron lung in a polio treatment center. Instead, she followed her own instincts and beliefs that the trick to overcoming the muscular weakening effect of the polio virus was exercise… lots of vigorous exercise.

She enrolled me in every kind of exercise class available in its day… ballet dancing, tap dancing, swimming, lifesaving, tumbling, and athletic competitive sports. Had I kept up at the tap dancing, I could have given Gene Kelly and Donald O'Connor a run for their money… NOT. By the time I stopped attending tap dancing classes, I knew my way around the ol' shuffle ball change on the hardwood dance floors, but I know of very few who could rise to the tap-dancing excellence and prowess of those two masters.

I was one of the lucky ones of my era who escaped the debilitating effects of the virus. Although I was somewhat limited by inadequate athletic abilities, I survived that episode in my early life, escaping incarceration in an iron lung, and spending instead an inordinate amount of time exercising. There are some poor souls who lived out their entire mortal existence in an iron lung. I recently read an online post reporting some folks who finally died after living in an iron lung for the majority of their lives. Paul Alexander, was paralyzed with polio at age 6 and relied on an iron lung machine to breathe until he took his final dying breath late in life at 78.

As noted in the Preface, I was influenced during my high school years by the poetry of Edgar Allan Poe, most notably by his romantic poem, "A Dream Within a Dream." I was fascinated by the possibility that you could have a dream within a dream while dreaming. I experimented with attempting lucid dreaming, but I never quite arrived at the ability to control or steer my dreams into more favorable realms and episodes. But the whole idea obviously provides the context for this present novel. I hope that it engenders positive, imaginative inspiration as you consider your own personal existence in mortality.